OTHER BOOKS BY SAME AUTHOR
– under the names of either
Tony Brennan or *Fr. Antony Brennan*:

The Bexford North Mysteries:

And the Dance Goes On

The Black Lamb

The Blight of Lady Emily

The Bell Tolled Twice

Death and the Lazy Milkmaid

Death and the Dowagers

***

Amaritudo

The Father

Cloistered Chronicles

The Greater Love

Ring Down the Curtain

***

<u>Short Stories:</u>

Is there Anyone There?

Simply This & Simply That!

***

<u>Trilogy</u>

Eminently Respectable Capers

Gertrude

Jumpin' Jerusalem! He's Back!

ISBN: 978-1-922788-54-2
Published by Vivid Publishing
P.O. Box 948, Fremantle
Western Australia 6959
www.vividpublishing.com.au

Cataloguing-in-Publication data is available from the National Library of Australia

RING DOWN THE CURTAIN

The rest is silence

TONY BRENNAN

'HAMLET' tragedy by William Shakespeare

NAMES OF UK COMPANY: ACTORS AND
BACKSTAGE STAFF

The Ghost (Hamlet's father): Dominic Oddfellow
8.Hamlet: Andrew Hammond-Oates
7.Claudius: Denis le Clerc
6.Laertes (Ophelia's brother): Lawrence Toohey
5.Gertrude: Mia Hinderspoken
4.Rosencrantz: William Smithers
3. Guildenstern: Albert Fellows
2.Ophelia: – Company actress; The Hon. Annabelle Nicholson
            (Daughter of Sir Harold Nicholson)
Replacement for Ophelia: Angela Cerney
1.Polonius: Sir Harold Nicholson
Horatio: Malcolm Mc Dermic
Fortinbras Prince of Norway: Alex Gardener.
(Horatio, Fortinbras and 'the Players' are the Only ones alive at
the end of the play.)
(Numbers indicate sequence of deaths in actual play)
AUSTRALIAN MANAGER OF 'The Elizabethan Theatre'
Newtown, Sydney: Mr James Cohen
ENGLISH MANAGER OF UK COMPANY: Mr George
Aspinall (in hospital)
Replacement: Mr Hiram Stotelmeyer.
Back stage staff: English Company employed: Charlie Wilks,
Jeremy Swift (Four professional technicians contracted to the
Australian 'Elizabethan Theatre'.)
The Players: Richard, Cecily, Roland, Margaret, Sweetheart,
York.

PROLOGUE

The curtain finally closed on the last poignant scene of the play. It rose again, one minute later, with all the cast ready on stage, and in their places, to take their bow.

There was a second of silence, then the air was filled with the sound of hundreds of patrons clapping furiously. Soon there was cheering and shouts of 'Bravo' with stamping of feet.

The actors kept their 'stage-faces' intact for the first of the bows. The back row came first in a corridor which opened up in the middle of the lines of actors and the least important actors in the play took the first bow.

They were enthusiastically applauded, then as they moved back to their allotted places on the stage, came the next group of more important actors.

The applause heated up, and...finally...the lead of the entire production, Andrew Hammond-Oates – the *Hamlet* of the play, took his solitary bow.

When he appeared, the crowd went wild. They shouted and cheered and called out their joy, at a performance that they would never, possibly, ever see the likes of, again.

At this ovation to the great actor, the cast joined in the applause; their carefully controlled faces now relaxed, and they were one with the audience in praising their brilliant hero, Hamlet himself!

Soon, the chanting changed as the audience realised, Ophelia was not present on stage. They shouted the name of 'Ophelia'.

From the stalls to the circle of the huge theatre, the cry went up:

'We want Ophelia'; 'We want Ophelia'; 'We want Ophelia'… …

The cast looked bewildered. They turned around to see where she could be.

In the wings there were standing only the Manager of the Company, George Aspinall, and the two stagehands belonging to the Company. They stood open mouthed; utterly helpless and totally bewildered. Everyone was asking: *Where could she be?*

Little did the crowd know they would never see Ophelia *alive* again.

***

Annie Watson hurried from the theatre urging her companion to walk faster. "Robert let's get out of this cold quickly. We're not young anymore. We can't take chills lightly…we're fragile beings now."

Bob Peters laughed. "That will really be the day when you are a fragile being, Annie. Why, watching you tearing along the street on this cold, dark night, you would swear you were no older than…" he flinched, as he noticed the withering glance Annie was giving him, and remembered, quickly, "thirty-seven at the most".

"Just as well, Bob Peters…just as well. Yes, that's my age for this year, anyhow.

"I went grey very early. Strange really; I've always eaten carrots."

"Carrots? What have they to do with it?"

"I've no idea, really. I read something about delaying the onset of going grey by eating some awful things, including carrots. I wasn't going to risk the other things, so I settled for what I knew – and what I like to eat, anyway."

She tossed her head of heavy grey hair. "Where, for goodness's sake, are all the taxis tonight? …Never mind, we'll walk to the station; it will do us good after sitting so long.

"We can begin the interrogation. Tell me, what did you think of Hamlet? –*himself*, the character - not the whole play."

"To be honest with you, Annie, I wanted to give him a

good clip over the ear. If he felt so badly about his mother and the usurper, Claudius, why did he take so long to ponder whether he should go ahead, and do it, or not. I wanted to yell out, as he faced the bare bodkin, 'Go ahead and get it over with…I want to go to the Loo'. "

In spite of herself, Annie laughed. "Look, I've told you before, Robert. With these long plays, you have to make sure you go to the bathroom, before the show begins. Otherwise, you face a difficult and painful evening."

She shook her head. "I can't understand why men can't understand that; women are aways aware of such problems."

"All right, Annie. I'll try to remember… I promise…"

"All right. I'll remind you each time, as I know you'll forget. Now, I want real feedback about the characters. What about Ophelia? Did you like the character…her presentation of the part. I know you have read the play, so you should have a good idea about Ophelia."

Bob Peters slowed his walk. "Annie, I truly thought she was the loveliest creature I have ever seen. She was, I think the word is, *ethereal*. She seemed to float across the floor; her complete innocence was palpable, whereas Gertrude was a sensuous, middle-aged woman …but, Annie, why wasn't Ophelia included in the curtain calls? She was the best of all of them."

"That surprised me, also, Bob. Not only the crowd wanted her, but the cast as well. I wonder what happened. Of course, she could have had a slight nervous reaction, when it was all over, and could have fainted; or, like you, had to go to the loo. She had been on stage for many hours, if not *on*, then waiting to go on. It's easy to forget that actors are human beings, and just like us.

"But go back to telling me your impressions of her performance. So, you really liked her, did you?"

"Well Annie, for me - a complete ignoramus - Ophelia stole my heart. She was ENTRANCING! I actually felt like weeping, when we saw her lying dead in the stream... Annie, how did they work that?"

"I was interested in that, illusion too, Bob. I think they use a full sheet of glass which they angled, with meticulous precision from the horizontal - the technicians up in the flies would be responsible for that. They tilted it so that we would actually think we were looking down at the stream... But, regardless of the trickery, I agree with you. In the pretend water, with her hair floating in the movement of the water, I thought it was possibly the most beautiful face I have ever seen, and for your reasons, exactly. Bob.

"Did you recognize her?"

"Recognize her? I don't understand...Wait! ...Never mind that! A taxi is coming..." Bob Peters rushed to the edge of the pavement and waved madly. "Look Annie, he's stopping."

A few minutes later they were on their way to the Railway Station.

"You are a sudden man, Bob Peters," commented Annie.

The ex-policeman smiled wryly. "Not really, Annie. I was trying to avoid a further discussion on 'Hamlet'. I had a wonderful, very enjoyable night, so I think 'Hamlet' must have been pretty damn good."

"But we had an agreement, Bob, and you are not getting out of it for one minute. You wanted to know all the great things you had missed in your education – the cultural things - and I, who was fortunately enough to have opportunities you didn't, promised to do what you asked me: to help fill in the blanks.

"We made an agreement and I'm sticking to my part, and - so help me – you are too."

"I've got a big mouth…"

"True."

"Well, you didn't have to agree so readily."

Annie laughed, then gave a sudden shout of fear, as the taxi driver swerved abruptly, practically standing on the brakes.

He came to a dead stop facing the footpath.

"Sorry, folks," he shouted. "There's a body lying on the street; nearly ran over it."

Horns blasted the night, there was the sound of an ambulance siren, people were screaming, and then a series of crashes as car, after car, smashed into one another, trying desperately hard to stop, or to get out of the chaos.

As soon as the cab was still, the driver turned around in his seat.

"Look, a word of advice. Get out now, and just disappear; you could be held up here for hours while the police, and all the official bods investigate the problem – whatever the problem is."

Bob Peters thanked the man for his advice, fumbling for his wallet.

The driver smiled and winked. "Don't worry about paying. This is not your fault, and you are not to blame, so just hop out now while the chaos is still bewildering."

Bob went to protest, but received a prod in the ribs from Annie, who using her beautiful voice, spoke to the very young driver.

"You are a very kind young man; your mother is very lucky to have you."

The driver actually blushed. "I'll tell her you said that!"

***

The accident, or whatever had happened, was only about twelve feet in front of their taxi. Their driver had been very clever in avoiding the body. He watched as the two elderly people left his cab.

The two friends were anxious to get out of the cold, but they naturally looked at the accident scene, as they passed.

Peters noticed the signs and spoke softly. "Annie, it's a crime scene. Obviously, someone has been killed."

Annie paused and said quickly. "God have mercy on them", and then made a small sign of the cross on her breast.

At that moment police moved away from the dead body lying on the road; their powerful hand-held lights lighting up the body in merciless clarity.

Annie glanced at the body, paused, then screamed, loudly.

"No. No. No! *Please God, NO!*" Peters looked at her bewildered.

"Annie, what the hell …?"

Annie had run out into the middle of the road and was standing at the side of the body, looking down, crying almost uncontrollably.

The police went to take hold of this obviously distraught woman.

Annie reacted, violently. "Don't you dare lay one hand on me. I know the victim, she is my neighbour…her name is Angela Cerney and lives at, 'The Forge', Bexford North. Her parents are the finest people I know; they adore this child…for child is all she is."

Peters had reached Annie by this time. He thought she had been mistaken, but when he heard the name and then the address, he staggered. A police Inspector came to his side. "It's not Superintendent Peters, is it?"

"Unfortunately, yes," muttered Peters.

He moved away from the local police, and went to Annie, holding her with his arm around her shoulders. "Dear God, Annie. This will kill that wonderful man, her father… but, Annie, why in the name of heaven, is she dressed like Ophelia? It couldn't be, could it?"

Annie, close to hysterics, whispered, "Yes."

The wig had partially come from girl's head and the face…the face…Peters turned to the local Inspector. "Inspector, quickly note that this body has been dead for only a very short time. We saw this woman in the Shakespearean play, 'Hamlet'. She was playing the part of Ophelia – that's why she is dressed like that; she's still in her stage costume - we saw her on stage less than 40 minutes ago; that body has been dead for a very short time …"

He staggered, and Annie quickly came to his support.

She spoke quickly, and with authority, to the Inspector.

"Get one of your portable chairs. The Retired Superintendent needs to sit down; he's had a severe and terrible shock."

The Inspector suggested the two witnesses sit in the police car, which they did with relief. Peters slumped down in the seat, his head in his hands. Annie sat with her arms around the distraught man; her tears mingling with his. She then sat up quickly.

"Bob, why was all that rubbish scattered around the body?

"I think the body's dropped off a garbage truck, or one of those metal bins they use for large amounts...they're called 'skips', I think. Please God, that isn't so; it is...*blasphemy*, if that's what it is."

Peters closed his eyes in anguish. "Annie, I never even noticed the rubbish: I had such a shock. But that would make sense. If she was killed in the playhouse – as she would likely have been - then they had to get rid of the body and they would have a lot of rubbish there as well, so it's more than likely that they would use one of those metal skips..."

Annie finished the sentence, "...which have to be collected and taken away by a heavy truck with a winching arrangement. The truck must have stopped suddenly, and the body has fallen out," finished Annie in a whisper.

Suddenly, Annie jumped out of the car. "Inspector," she called in her most authoritative voice. "Keep those actors at the playhouse; don't let them go home. This could, and most probably did, happen there; the body then dumped out here where it could easily be accounted for as a road victim. I think it has fallen from a garbage truck when it stopped suddenly." She raised herself on her toes. "Yes, I see. There are traffic lights just ahead of the body. It's possible, the truck stopped with a jerk, and with the sudden movement, the body - which could have been near the top - simply toppled out onto the road." She moved closer and forced herself to study the body.

"Inspector, get your police surgeon here at once; he should have been here already. The body has a broken arm, I think. It is lying at an impossible angle: it has happened 'post-mortem'. Dear God, the monster who set this in motion is, I suspect, just sitting at his, or her, ease in the playhouse."

The local sergeant was angry; the last thing he wanted was a nosey, 'know-it-all outsider'. He mumbled something about not knowing of any 'playhouse'.

Annie spoke louder: "What do you mean, Sergeant, 'which playhouse?'

"Inspector, transfer this ignorant Sergeant from your team. We are in Newtown and the only playhouse here is the famous 'Elizabethan Theatre', and he doesn't even know of it." She lowered her head and spoke to Peters.

"Bob, do you think you could come back with me to the theatre? I just want to see the company before they go home…"

The local Inspector tried to calm the situation, which was

arising. Bloody Hell, with this weird death, it was already complex enough – an actress lying dead in the middle of a city street. The driver of the taxi, who had ended up with his car on the pavement, had his head in his hands. obviously suffering from shock; but thank God, he'd managed to miss the body with, literally, inches between it and the corpse ...and now...what?

The inspector was well aware he was left with a very dumb sergeant and a fairly new, very young constable.

His mind was racked with questions, as to what he was supposed to do next; he had only recently been promoted to Inspector, and was feeling his way, with a vengeance, on questions of protocol.

The last thing he needed was a clash with an imperious woman.

***

The inspector made a decision. He realised there was only one thing to do, *that he could do* – make use of the Superintendent - so quickly running to the other door of the police car, he opened it and spoke to the retired Superintendent.

"Sir, would you help me...er... with your companion, of course? My name's Scully. I'm not sure what I am to do. I'm new to the rank, sir."

With a sigh, Bob Peter climbed out of the car. He tried to control himself and took hold of Annie's arm. "Hush, Annie. Inspector Scully has a fearful job. Give him a break, please..."

"But Bob, he'll get away."

"Who?"

"The murderer from the playhouse."

"Why should he happen to be from there, Annie?" Annie, frustrated at such stupidity, ran her fingers through her enormous crop of grey hair sending it cascading down on her shoulders. "You men…you men. No wonder a young woman is afraid to go out on the streets in this evil city…

"Look, Bob. It's abundantly clear. Would anyone in their right senses wander through the streets dressed in her diaphanous nightwear, with bare feet and an obvious wig, with hair to her waist? She's been put here from someone in the company; obviously it was too dangerous for the body to be found in the playhouse."

Inspector Scully broke into this conversation. "Madam, that is not quite correct. A prostitute would quite likely adopt such a disguise and wander the street dressed as you describe…"

That statement roused Peters, more than Annie's had. "Hold your tongue, Inspector. You are referring to a totally innocent, and sinless young woman, whom we both know intimately. She has been part of our lives for nearly twenty years. Mrs Watson lives opposite her, and I live next to her."

"That's at this Bexford North place, is it?"

"Yes, and you asked me for assistance, well, for goodness' sake get in touch with Superintendent Manders, or Inspector Watkins, at Tavistock Police Station…they'll confirm all I've said, but please, please do as Mrs Watson's suggested: try to keep that company of players together. You'll need to question all the main ones tonight before they can concoct some rigmarole by tomorrow... Dear God! We have wasted 30 minutes already if we delay any further the whole place will be deserted..."

The local inspector grabbed this suggestion of what to do.

"Right, Sir, I'll attend to that right away. Could I ask you to remain, both of you with me, until I've gone to the play-house?" He looked embarrassed. "We don't have another car..."

"Just get in and we'll be off," shouted Peters.

The sergeant looked terrified at the thought of being left alone at the scene. The Inspector turned and spoke to the constable: 'Listen son, there's a telephone in that shop that's still open. Ring from there and send for the ambulance to take the body away to the morgue; ring the Police Doctor, and when he gets here, say I demand an autopsy on the dead woman; get him to have a look at the taxi driver – see if he can help him; then try to find a way around these smashed vehicles and get the traffic flowing again. That is vital.

"If you finish all that, and I haven't returned, come to me at the Elizabethan. You'll have to run; the bastard - I mean - the Superintendent – the drunken slob - took the other car. Right?" As the Inspector turned away, he spoke over his shoulder. "And you didn't hear that remark about the Superintendent, Ok?"

The constable was writing furiously as his superior spoke, then said, simply: "Don't worry Inspector, it will all be done, sir and I'll join you, if you are still at the theatre. I know where it is."

The Inspector jumped into the driving seat, put on his siren and made an illegal turn and drove furiously back to the Theatre. In the back seat, Peters raised his eyebrows at his companion. "What did that good man, your husband, Mr Watson, say about you, Annie. 'You were always 'finding bodies.' Well, he certainly knew you. I thought I was finished with all of that."

"I'm sorry, Bob. I could not stay quiet, when one of the loveliest young women I have ever known, has been murdered, perhaps right before our eyes…and I didn't do anything about it.

"But never mind all that now, Bob. Cast your mind back to your memory of the actress, Ophelia, as you watched the play. You said you were entranced by Ophelia; think through every action she performed; the contacts she made with another actor, whether she accepted a drink from another player, or appeared to stagger, at any time…anything you can remember about her performance…the whole time. She is often on stage but not for very long scenes; they were fairly short scenes really. There is that fairly long scene with Hamlet, where he cruelly tells her to '*Get thee to a nunnery and quickly too, farewell*'. But I have to admit that when Ophelia goes mad, there is a lot of movement from her. I can't really remember all of that. I suspect that the actress is given a fair amount of freedom in interpreting the really 'insane-scenes.'"

Peters had his eyes on the route they were taking and was aware that they had reached the theatre, before Annie had. The car stopped suddenly, and the Inspector was ready to jump out to speak to a gravely disturbed man in a dinner suit with a starched white front - quite obviously the Theatre Manager. He was clearly very upset and advanced on the police car.

Annie quickly held on to the Inspector's sleeve and spoke softly. "One moment, Inspector. The dead girl is named Angela Cerney, that is, spelled C.E.R.N.E.Y., but it is pronounced, CARNEY. They wouldn't know whom you meant if you said it, as it is spelt. The theatre would know her only as *Carney*. Is that clear?"

The policeman nodded. "Yes Madam, thank you; I really appreciate you telling me that," and opened the door of the car and went to meet the Manager.

The Manager began speaking, before the Inspector, had even left the car. "Thank God, Officer, you've arrived. I've nearly gone mad with worrying ever since they came to tell me that Angela was dead."

"*Who*, told you that, sir, and *when*?"

The manager looked bewildered at the question.

"Mrs Higgs, and her cleaning company, of course – they were coming to work: they clean here after every performance. They arrived just when the first of the actors were ready to leave. Mrs Higgs, herself, saw the body of the poor young woman lying on the street. And, to our utter astonishment, she said she was dead."

"You were surprised?"

The Theatre manager stared at the police officer. "Of course, I was surprised!" he snapped. "A world-famous

Theatre company from the UK is here to give us the best of British Drama, and a young Australian actress dies after the show… and when", he added, in anguish, "she'd given the performance of a lifetime in her glorious role of Ophelia."

The middle-aged man's voice began to crack and wobble. "Forgive me, Officers, Angela was a favourite with the cast. They were so glad to get her when the actress brought out from England, with the cast to play the role, became ill, and was forced to cancel; so, the Australian amateur had to take on the demanding role.

"We were so worried about the child – that is how I thought of Angela: a pure and innocent child – yet she gave a far greater performance than the official actress brought out from England."

Annie and Peters had emerged from the car. Annie immediately asked: "And just where are the cast members now? What have you done with them?"

The Inspector took the hint. "Yes, indeed, that is what we want to know? Are they still in the Theatre?

"Sir and Madam, they are all here and are on the stage where there is a phone you could use, in the wings; I know you'll need one.

"Come in, please. Come and speak to the cast; there have been hysterics, tears galore and one, older, woman, who plays Gertrude, actually fainted."

Annie took Bob Peters' arm and, as they retraced their steps into the Theatre, Annie was muttering under her breath: never again, no matter what my lady Penelope Sheridan has to say about it. Walking in these three- inch heels, is no joke at my age. She forced herself to concentrate on the stage.

The cast looked to have about 20 members gathered together on the stage, but Annie realised all the technical staff and ancillary staff – the makeup experts, wardrobe staff, the prompts - would be there, as well as the actors. There appeared to be, twelve or thirteen actors, perhaps more, altogether.

She knew there were only eleven major roles in the play, but perhaps the Lead actor might have to bring his understudy with him, just in case something went wrong.

She was interested to see that the actors were very ordinary human beings: they were very tired and looked it. Without their brilliant make-up and glorious costumes, they looked just like the crowd you would find at a shopping mall who had finished working for the day.

The Police Inspector didn't introduce either Peters or Annie… wisely, they both thought. He introduced himself and made a simple, yet genuine, apology for keeping them from their rest after their long hours of performing.

The actors were sitting on a variety of seats, some genuine chairs, but most of them just anything they could find – most of the men were sitting on the floor. Hamlet, being the big star of the show, had sole use of the throne which– within the play - was used by Claudius.

The Inspector began by giving a detailed account of where the body had been found; the circumstances of the multiple car crashes that nearly destroyed the body. He then described his discovery of the identity of the victim, by her costume – which Annie applauded silently. It was a clever way around telling the cast, that it was found and identified by a lay-woman and a Superintendent of Police, now retired.

While he was talking, both Annie and Peters were studying the actor, who played the lead role.

Hamlet was, indeed, surprisingly enough, even more handsome, than he had appeared in the performance – he was, what could even be called, 'beautiful'. He was tall, at least six feet tall, with perfect features, truly large and beautiful eyes, a straight nose, and perfect gleaming skin. His lips were wide and well-shaped and were a slightly rosy colour which hinted at suppressed passion, while surrounding this face was a full head of very blond hair, slightly longer than usual, but completely correct for the period, and the country: Annie reminded herself, Hamlet was Prince of *Denmark* – they all seemed to be blonde in the Scandinavian countries.

Annie turned her attention then to Gertrude. Something was wrong there. That woman, she thought, is very worried. Why? She asked herself; she could be emotionally shattered, even furious at being kept out of bed, or being upstaged by lesser characters but, no, she was definitely *worried*… unusual…worth noting. And Annie felt sure, the worry concerned the young woman holding onto her arm, a pretty, slim, long-haired girl, with beautiful eyes.

Annie's attention was suddenly riveted on the young actress. Why was she frowning, as if angry? And why was she dressed as Ophelia? She was determined to find out!

Annie clapped her hands sharply and spoke authoritatively: "As I point to each one of you, kindly tell us your real name, then the part you play in this glorious Shakespearean play." In an aside she spoke quietly to Peters. "Bob, keep a note of all this," and pointed a long finger at the woman she had identified as, "Gertrude."

The woman immediately began to tremble, then in a loud voice, forced herself to speak:

"My name is Mia Hinderspoken; I play Gertrude, the wife…" Annie interrupted brusquely. "No elaboration, thank you; we are totally familiar with the play…Next? "

A tremulous old voice declared himself to be:

"Sir Harold Nicholson, mam, I was… Polonius". He looked ill.

And so, it went on.

"Dominic Oddfellow…I am the Ghost of Hamlet's father". How odd, Annie thought it all was; Dominic looked the sort that could take on the role of an elderly vicar; he had a venerable look about him – a 'churchy' look.

"Denis le Clerc…I am the villain, Claudius." He, indeed, looked the villain, Annie thought. You wouldn't trust a young girl – or, she thought briefly, a young man - anywhere near this character. She moved on.

"Lawrence Toohey. I'm Laertes, brother of Ophelia."

"Malcolm Mc Dermic. I am the faithful friend, Horatio"

"*And are, you?*" Annie asked quickly, surprising the actor who had to stand up again. "As a matter of fact, mam … um…yes…yes; I suppose I am."

The very attractive young star, and leading man of the

show, rose slowly to his feet; Annie was aware of the beauty of the movement. She spoke first.

"According to the placards outside this theatre, you are Andrew Oates. Is that right?"

"Actually, it is Hammond hyphen Oates, mam, but I prefer, when touring, outside the UK, to just use a simple form of the name. If I may be permitted to make a personal remark, you speak beautifully, Madam."

"How very kind of you… Next!"

"Rosencrantz. And in my other life, I am William Smithers. I am one of the two sent to London who end up swinging from a noose, with my…"

"friend", interposed Annie, "who is called Guildenstern sitting there," and Annie pointed to another young man who was yawning, widely. She spoke – her voice like ice. "I'm so sorry, if we are interrupting your beauty sleep." The man stood up quickly.

"Sorry, mam. Yes, I am Guildenstern. My name is Albert Fellows."

Annie pointed to the last man sitting with the actors. "And you must be Fortinbras, Prince of Norway. What is your real name?"

"Alex Gardener, mam."

"And now, the stagehands," Annie's eyes swept over the stage; she saw two men in dungarees. "Would the stagehands please stand up. Two men immediately stood up.

The taller of the two, spoke. "There are only two, myself …"

"And you are?"

"Charlie Wilks, mam. The only other one is Jeremy Swift. There are more, of course, but four of them belong to this Theatre. They are experts and do all the pushing of buttons that lift huge sets into the ceiling, and lower the same, throughout the play. They also managed the lights and such. They use all the codes and abbreviations that the Company brought with them from England. They are the professionals in this field; Jeremy and I are the trained workmen, who do all the hard work on the stage itself. We have really nothing to do with the experts. They are engaged for the length of the season, by this theatre. I don't even know their names, but the Theatre Manager would."

"That's a full and sensible reply. Thank you, Charlie."

Annie then consulted a non-existent list in her hand and then said: "Well that's the lot…no, wait a minute. I think I've forgotten a minor part…Oh, yes, Ophelia? Stand up Ophelia and tell me your real name."

The young woman holding onto the arm of Gertrude, stood up, her face burning at the insult she had received.

"So pleased you could find time to get around to the trash that is left, Mam. You must remind me to get you an invite to the palace, when I return home."

"How lovely, child; I'll look forward to it," Annie replied. "That is, of course, if you are permitted to go back to your native land. But, just in case we do let you go, what is your name…" her voice sharpened: it was cold and incisive. "Immediately, and without any added comments, or else we would have to take you to the police station for wasting the time of the police." The girl looked startled and mumbled:

"Annabelle Nicholson".

"Poor diction, as well. Ah well! And you, the daughter of the great Sir Harold Nicholson, who plays Polonius!" She turned to the Inspector. "Inspector, I notice your excellent Constable is back again. Would you set him to take the names of the Australian-based stagehands, or perhaps 'Technicians' would be a better word. We already have Charlie and Jeremy."

She addressed the stage again. "All those who were not actors in the play move to one side of the stage; that would make clear to the police all the workers whom the audience never sees, but without whom, no show would ever go on." She suddenly realised someone vital was missing.

"But where is the Company Manager who would have travelled with you to bring you to this country? Why is he missing?" Her eyes found the Australian manager of the playhouse sitting in the front stalls. He rose to his feet.

"I'm sorry, madam. I meant to tell you. Mr George Aspinall, the Company's manager, was taken by ambulance to Emergency, when he heard the terrible news of the death. They think, at the hospital, he's had a stroke.

"He's in hospital? Dear God!" She turned to the Inspector. "I'm sure you would give orders, Inspector, that the patient must be in a private room and that a constable must be seated at the patient's door, day and night – no one is permitted to see him, especially members of this cast. Just inform the hospital this is a serious police inquiry involving, as seems certain, the crime of *murder*."

At the sound of that word, the actors were startled and

shocked. Most of the women on the stage, and one of the men, began to weep. The most affected was Gertrude, she sobbed aloud. Both Polonius and the young woman, the Company Ophelia, tried to comfort her.

Annie had not finished startling the Inspector. "Of course, Inspector you would have realised you will need to notify the Police Commissioner of this.

"The Australian Theatre manager will have to inform the Governor-General of Australia who represents her Majesty. He is resident either here in Sydney, or in Canberra. He will notify the British Embassy in Canberra. Canberra might be better - at this time of night. With the cast being British citizens, we now have an international incident – potentially criminal. This will be reported in all the news outlets in London tomorrow morning."

The Inspector looked startled at Annie's warning, then rallied and lied convincingly. "Yes, it has been all done as you suggested. I have also petitioned for more men; we must have more men to cope with this case. The field is such a large one and the case is wide open."

He now noticed - what Annie had noticed earlier - with great relief, his constable had arrived and was sitting quietly waiting for him; he rushed to the young man. There followed a frantic conversation between the Inspector and the Constable. The constable listened carefully, nodded his head – taking notes all the time, and then ran for the telephone in the wings of the stage where there was a useful big, and full, Telephone Directory. He quickly sorted through the early pages of the Directory to find all the very important Government and vice-regal numbers. Once found, he began dialling the numbers he needed.

Peters spoke privately to the Inspector. "Ring Tavistock police station, Inspector, I beg you. Once you mention my name and the name of Annie Watson, the Superintendent there, Manders, will immediately come to our assistance and you couldn't have a better team than what he has.

"This is the seventh murder I have worked on with Mrs Watson; it was she who solved every one of the hideous cases we had. I got all the credit; she did all the work. And they were truly dreadful crimes too. She is a famous criminologist…quite famous."

Annie went back to the front stalls, where the Constable was sitting after he had finished telephoning. "Constable, I've forgotten something. Could you find out the name of the Theatre Manager *here* – the one I've been talking to. I clean forgot to ask him and we need it. Can you do it, surreptitiously, and then write it on a small piece of paper and slip it to me? And a second thing: did you get the morgue's assurance that there would be a full autopsy of the child's body? We need to know the contents of the dead girl's stomach."

"I'll ring the morgue again, Madam. I did tell them that. I'll reinforce the order and also tell them we are waiting for a result and to notify the Inspector immediately when the findings are available. I'll stress the fact that, as you said, just now, this is an international event now."

"Thank you. I'm nearly certain it is poison, but one that takes possibly up to an hour, or there-abouts, to take effect…

that of course would depend on the quantity taken; the science bods should be able to find the amount indicated in the stomach of the deceased." She turned away, then turned back, "and would you please tell me your name, Constable. I am very impressed by your work this night…"

"Thank you, Madam. My name is Mark le Breton."

"Thank you, Constable le Breton. Now, you won't forget the request for the name of the Australian Theatre Manager?"

"Consider it done!" The constable smiled. Two minutes later Annie saw him go onto the stage and was soon speaking with the Manager.

She breathed a sigh of relief. Fancy forgetting that; age is telling, she thought. She was suddenly aware of how tired she was; she needed to sit down but was afraid to do so as she could easily fall asleep.

Constable le Breton came to Annie and bent down and seemed to pick up a page of note paper. "Excuse me, Madam, I think you dropped this." He held out the note.

"Why, so I did. You are an observant young man. Thank you." She smiled. Her eyes followed the constable. That youngster will go far… She then resumed reading the note just given to her: the Australian Theatre Manager's name was 'James Cohen' – that's a strange mixture!

She went to Peters quickly. "Bob, where is the cast staying? Which Hotel? Please God it is the same place. Once they are allowed to go, they must remain in the hotel with police at all the exit places.

"That's going to be difficult, Annie…"

"Doesn't matter. Until they have all been thoroughly interviewed by the police, they are all suspects. They have no legal leg to stand on." She went to sit down, then stood up quickly having just remembered something vital. She called out in a loud voice. "Mr Cohen! Mr Cohen! Where in heavens' name are the Players?

"In the play, *within the play*, there were six actors there performing last night, so where have they disappeared to... and why haven't you reminded us of them. Why are they not here?"

The Theatre Manager, struggled to get out his chair quickly. "I'm terribly sorry, Madam. It slipped my mind altogether. Please let me explain. My mistake was not intentional.

"The Players do not belong to the Company; they are sub-contracted to the Company, but only for the short time they are on stage here. They wait until the end of the play, to take their bow, then go on home to the hotel.

"They really are like strangers to most of the company cast. Hamlet, of course, and Laertes have dealings with them and many of the cast are there watching the play which illustrates the poisoning of the previous king and confirms Hamlet's suspicions, but I don't think many of the big cast even know the players' names."

Annie snapped: "Regardless of their names, we want them back here in a flash." She turned to Constable le Breton. "Constable, ring the hotel – get the number from Mr Cohen, and tell them they must come immediately back to the theatre: the police demand it. They might not even know of the death. Tell them to get cabs but to get here quickly... or we'll come and get them!" The constable ran back to the telephone in the wings. Within five minutes he was able to inform Annie that the Players were already on the way and that they had no idea of Angela' death.

***

Peters who had remained silent in Annie's questioning of the staff, now took an active role. "Mr Oates, you had, I think, more time spent with Ophelia than anyone else. Did you notice anything wrong during the performance? Did the actress appear at all frightened, or worried, or did she stumble in any section?"

The great man stood up. "Sir, let me say this publicly, once and for all. It was an absolute delight to play opposite her. She had no stupid, unrehearsed movements of voice, or body. She played it straight as the script demanded and thus it was, for me, one of the best nights of our Australian tour. I was not trying to mend situations which I had been led into by a fumbling, embarrassingly ignorant, actress, who has no idea of innocence or, indeed, any understanding of the character she was playing.

"Tonight, was a sheer delight. I wanted to kiss that beautiful, fragile, child for the experience, which I don't think I'll ever have again. For me, Angela was perfection – not only as an actress of unbelievable talent and grace, but as a young woman with the character of an angel – as indeed her name indicates."

This ovation was delivered with such sincerity and force, that Annie was close to tears. Many of the actors present actually clapped as the beautiful voice of the star left everyone breathless.

***

As Annie was just about to seek information regarding the garbage skip, the players came hurriedly into the theatre. Constable le Breton brought them immediately to Annie.

The first thing that Annie noticed was that all six of the Players were, or had been, crying. Annie took them to a back part of the stalls and demanded that the electrician turn on the lights for them.

With the lights, Annie could see the six actors clearly. The oldest of them was a tall, fine-looking man, who introduced himself as Richard York. He then introduced each of the others who, it turned out, were all part of the same family... his wife, Cecily, his son, Roland, Roland's wife, Margaret, and their daughter, Sweetheart.

Annie spoke, clearly unsure, exactly how to proceed. "Mr York, I am very happy to meet your family. I am Mrs Watson, I am assisting the police in this enquiry into the death of the young woman, Angela Cerney who, as you would well know, was the Ophelia in this great play. The constable told us you didn't even know of the death...I'm sorry to have been the person to alarm you so greatly."

The older woman, Cecily spoke. "No, mam, I thank God, you did enlighten us. That precious girl was the most beautiful, fragile child, I have ever watched on the stage."

Her, husband interrupted. "But, Mrs Watson, we are in a rather peculiar situation in regard to the other players in the play. Could I ask Roland, my son, to explain this to you?"

"Of course. you may, Mrs York," Annie smiled. "I'm intrigued actually." She looked carefully at this man, Roland. This member of the family looked like a successful businessman and was, she guessed, in his forties.

"Mam, I'm Roland, and, yes, in a way, I suppose it is intriguing. To us, it is totally normal.

"We are a private, separate company, and we are subcontracted to the big Company which produces the whole play. We are a small company, who hire ourselves out to, not only Drama Companies, but also to Opera Companies. You would realise, that just about every professional production – either Drama or Opera - has the need of 'non-speaking, or 'non-singing,' characters – for crowds, soldiers, guards, people in markets, streets, and so on.

"My father, Richard York, seized this business opportunity, decades ago, and we've built up a reputation for total honesty, and – more than anything else – *reliability* and so we are working nearly all the year in either Drama, or Opera.

"This work is quite extensive in 'Hamlet' as we have to follow Hamlet's directions – which of course, are Shakespeare's directions - on a simple little play – it's quite short, but requires a lot of rehearsal to get it perfect. In other performances, we often have to have to spend a couple of days to learn what we have to do, so we're used to that.

"In this play, our work finishes straight after the little play is finished. We usually just gather in the Green Room and wait until it is time to go for our bows. Then, we normally go home. Tonight, it was different..."

"Please tell me, Roland, why it was different?" Annie asked.

"Mam, we have seen Hamlet performed dozens of times in other cities in various parts of the UK. This time, we wanted to see what the great Andrew Hammond-Oates really was like, particularly how he coped with the difficult end part of the play - but we also were intrigued to find there was an *Australian* amateur taking the part of the Company Ophelia. We were naturally interested in seeing how she went in that most difficult role.

"It was really curiosity that made us stay and watch Ophelia from the wings. We were spellbound; we had never seen an Ophelia such as this one. We thought she was the most beautiful, soulful, sinless, example of womanhood that we would ever see on the boards. We left the theatre after Ophelia had been put in the stream..." Annie held up her hand.

"Just a moment, Roland. You said you and your family were going to watch this great actor Hammond-Oates and see how he coped with the gruesome end section of the play and now you are saying you left as soon as Ophelia had been put in the stream..."

"You're absolutely right, Mrs Watson. The answer is not sinister, but very simple. We were so emotionally drained by Ophelia's performance that the wife and our daughter asked if we could just 'cut' Hamlet's last scenes and, go home after the bows. That mean we went to the Green Room, as we usually did, and waited there so we would not miss our bows. Then we left the Theatre and went back to the hotel, talking all the time about the extraordinary actress we had been privileged to see.

"We argued we could see Hamlet any night of the year, whereas this amateur Ophelia, was only booked for the one night." He smiled at the irony of what he had just said. "We realised now, we have missed out, as there won't be another night for us to see Mr Hammond-Oates."

Cecily took up the tale from her son. "So, you see, mam, we were nearly hysterical with shock when we were told on the phone, by the Constable, that the Ophelia we saw, was dead! We couldn't believe it."

Annie reached out her hand and took the hand of the elderly woman. "Cecily, I do understand all you are saying. I actually was in the audience tonight, and I saw what you saw. I was stunned at the greatness of what I was seeing."

The young woman raised a tear-streaked face. "Mam, what happened, how did she die? – I still cannot believe it."

"That's what the police are trying to discover, and we ask you to help us…you might have some knowledge we do not have. We'll wait and see."

While she was speaking, Annie was studying the faces before her. She was convinced she was just wasting her time with this family. They were palpably innocent, as well as terribly shocked by the death. These were good people. An extraordinary good family, who spent their working life in the theatre, at either the Drama, or the Opera. What an exotic life! She never expected to find this phenomenon and was slightly thrown off balance by this new experience.

Her voice became crisp and strong. "Just a few more questions and we're through. I have to ask you if you have much intermingling with the regular Company members of the cast?"

Richard, the obvious head of the family, spoke firmly. "No, mam, we don't. It's not our fault; in general, we've found the regular actors regard themselves as superior to 'travelling actors'. If our ways cross, we are polite to each other, but neither they, nor we, ever try to make friendships with each other. Usually, straight after the bows, we leave the theatre and walk home. We usually go by the back door to avoid all the theatre patrons and we are back at the hotel in, sometimes, less than fifteen minutes. We generally have a light supper, then are well and truly ready, for bed."

"That's a sensible and full account of your routine, Richard, thank you. Now only two more questions and then I'll hand you over to Superintendent Robert Peters – he's a very good and kindly man; you have nothing to fear from him.

"Richard, I address my question to you, as head of the family, but if others want to reply, do so, by all means. Richard, in your time in this theatre last night, did you see anything amiss, anything that puzzled you, or troubled you; any disagreements, or arguments, in fact anything at all, 'out of place'?"

Richard York looked at his family. They each shook their heads. He turned to Annie with both hands open, and said sadly: "Nothing, mam, nothing at all. Everything was just as normal."

"Right! Now, did any of you, as you were all on last night, have a drink of the Health Food Drink that most actors were taking?"

Margaret, the wife of Roland, answered, rather bitterly. "No, Mrs Watson, they wouldn't ever offer it to us."

"How lucky you were, Margaret, thank God for that." Annie smiled.

She stood up and said briskly. "Wait here. I'm afraid you will have to stay with the regular actors now until this is all solved; you will be taken back to the hotel, when the others are permitted to go." She smiled naturally. "Thank you, each one of you. You have not only answered my questions, but you have let me into a secret aspect of stage work, I never knew before. Just wait here, Peters will be here directly."

***

Annie spoke briefly to Peters, explaining the situation with the Players. She told him her opinion of the family and advised him to go gently, as they were suffering from shock.

Superintendent Peters brought the 'Players' down to the front stalls and he spoke to them there.

Annie left him to the Players and went in search of the theatre manager.

She was well known as the one who kept her feet on the ground, on all occasions, so now, she spoke to the Australian Theatre manager, Mr James Cohen, and suggested he contact the hotel where the company was staying and ask them if they could rustle up a scratch supper, with plenty of tea and coffee –possibly more coffee than tea - and send it round to the Theatre. He could hint at the terrible accident that had occurred, and that the actors were all shaken, and needed refreshments, *NOW*, as it could be hours before they were allowed to return to the hotel.

The manager looked surprised at the suggestion but acted immediately. Within fifteen minutes, waiters from the Hotel were distributing refreshments to the cast and crew. Annie grabbed this opportunity of asking for advice from the manager, as to the stagehand, who would know about the rubbish collection, from the theatre, Mr Cohen suggested, a young man called, Charlie Wilks would be best on that.

"I've met Charlie. Please ask him to come here to me immediately, Mr Cohen."

Charlie was an energetic and youthful looking man. He leapt down from the stage to the floor of the stalls where Annie was standing. She thanked the man and asked him to take her to where the rubbish was disposed of from the theatre. They were soon walking smartly up the steps to the stage, then through a maze of passages to an outside, back door. When Charlie opened it, he let out a cry of dismay. "Oh, they've already been and collected the bin."

"Yes," calmly answered Annie. "I expected that. Do you have much rubbish from the theatre, Mr Wilks?"

"You wouldn't believe how much junk is left in a theatre, mam, and this is a very large building. There is a lot from the actors as well, but the main stuff comes from the stalls and the circle. But we – on this side of the curtain - need a lot of stuff delivered in big cardboard boxes, as well, for breakable things; that have to be replaced quickly, so we can easily fill a bin twice a week. Tonight, was one of the nights they collect."

"Mr Wilks, would you say most people would just toss the junk in without looking inside the bin?"

"Definitely, mam. Some of the stuff is stinking - you know – shi…I mean faeces, and such…"

"Goodness gracious me; I never knew that. And theatre goers leave rubbish behind them?"

"Piles of rubbish, mam. Makes sense really. No one wants to travel home with their arms full of empty boxes or even bottles…" At that word, Annie was truly astonished. "But drinking alcohol would never be allowed, would it?"

"Officially, no, mam, but there's many a group that smuggle in bottles of the hard stuff and leave the empty bottles when they leave."

"Thank you, Mr Wilkes; you might be required to repeat your information in a court of law, if ever this comes to court."

"I'd be happy to do that; anything to pay back the bastard – begging your pardon, mam – who has done this to little Angela."

Annie shook hands with this exemplary young man and returned to front of stage.

***

Arriving there she was just in time to see an actor stumble as if he were in danger of falling. She shouted a warning: "Quick, someone, catch Polonius. He's going to fall."

Her loud cry coincided with the arrival of the Superintendent Manders from Tavistock. He and his team came surging into the theatre.

Annie was unaware of their arrival.

Several cast members, alerted to the state of the older man, rushed to his aid, but were too late. Annie shouted again. "Stand away from the body...one person, check his breathing. If there is none, see if CPR is possible." She hurried to the patient, and as she reached Polonius, violent vomiting occurred, then diarrhea, then the body lay still. The actors moved away, embarrassed...uncertain.

Annie moved away, and stated, sadly: "I'm sorry. Polonius is dead". She made the sign of the cross.

There was a concerted cry of unbelief from the actors. "He's only fallen...He's an old man...He'll be all right..." only to be followed by the real Ophelia, who screamed piercingly: "*My God, she's right. My father is dead...he's dead! ... My father's dead!*".

She fell to her knees beside the body, crying helplessly. Gertrude wept as loudly, as the daughter.

Peters had run up the stairs to the stage and checked the body. Yes, he was certain the old actor was dead. He shouted to the Inspector: "Ring the Police surgeon at once. He must be here. He should have been here earlier."

He then saw Manders, for the first time. "Thank God you're here Super. Take over; the other one's gone missing" he lowered his voice as Manders came near: "Dead drunk! ... We need as many men as you can give us. I'll clear it all with the Commissioner."

"Right sir, coming up." He turned to Inspector Watkins. "Watkins get all the names: their real ones and the people they played in this tragedy…

Annie intervened. "Inspector Watkins, we have all of those. Peters has a copy; he could give it to you. Superintendent and Inspector Watkins, the constable here is first class; he has a mine of information to give you regarding the death of the actress; of the Manager of the Company who's been rushed to the hospital; of the autopsy on Ophelia's body which is underway; and of the Governor-General and the British Embassy who have both been notified - as you would recognize instantly: all the cast being British, this is now an international crime." She staggered a little. "I'm sorry, I need to sit down."

Superintendent Manders had great respect for Annie. He rushed to her and helped her to a seat in the stalls. He treated her tenderly; well aware she was no longer young. They had been friends for many years now. "Just sit still, Mrs Watson. You've had a terrible evening…" He turned to his sergeant. "Inspector Watkins show those rotten newspapers to Mrs Watson."

"Sir, coming up!" The sergeant handed the papers to Annie who scanned the headlines swiftly: "I was waiting for this one," she said, bitterly.

'THE POMS KILL AUSSIE OPHELIA IN
THEATRE MYSTERY'

The second one worried her more:

VICTIM'S FATHER VOWS VENGEANCE

"I'LL KILL THE BASTARD"

"Oh, please God, don't let the family see that one!" Annie cried. The last two were fairly harmless: they obviously had nothing at all alarming to say:

'FAMILY BESIEGED BY PRESS.'

'A MURDERER ON THE LOOSE IN NEWTOWN'

Annie forced herself to stop reading and reached out to hold onto the Superintendent's arm. "But Super…how can I ever face the parents again?

"Remember, they live opposite me, and next to Bob Peters; we are personally involved. This will kill Reg and Susan; their precious first-born child… and what a child… *murdered!* …Yes, it will kill them…Oh, I can't bear it." For the first time, Annie's self-control broke, and she hid her face and wept. Manders signalled to his constable and sent him to Annie.

Annie looked up at her grandson, Constable Sheridan. He held out his arms and took his precious grandmother in a strong embrace. "Lady Ann, just take it easy. The *real police* are here, now!" He smiled, teasing her, knowing she would react, dramatically, to that insult.

Now, Annie, truly emotionally upset, as she undoubtedly was, had no intention of letting the young brat get away with that. "*Real police*. We'll see what you are capable of now that I'm watching you! You are all shining buckles and buttons at the moment – fresh from your graduation ceremony at Goulburn - but that will soon wear off when you're facing a real situation. We'll then see if there's anything inside the outer shell.

"Let me warn you, sonny, if you do not retract that libellous statement, I'm leaving my millions to another of my grandchildren."

Bernard, the second eldest child of Annie's daughter, the Lady Penelope Sheridan, had a good sense of humour. Aware of how poor Annie actually was, he mimed dreadful shock, clutched his breast, went down on one knee and removed his cap.

"Now, that scares me to death; it really terrifies me, so I'll retract it immediately". He struck his breast saying brokenly: "*mea culpa, mea culpa, mea maxima culpa!*" He stood up. "Is that enough?" He started to laugh "Tell me, *Grannie*, are you quite finished giving your imitation of a frail, wimpy, girl? If you are, could you help a young copper, with a bit of inside dope?"

"Wait till I've seen your lady mother…I'll … …No, let's stop this charade, Bernard…"

"Have you seen Reg and Susan? I can't bear to think of them, or I'll crack up completely." The young Constable's face went white. "It was terrible, Lady Ann. Seeing the family just after Sergeant Clarkson had informed them of the death, was the hardest thing I have ever done. Reg is beside himself with grief and spent a whole hour smashing his big hammer on the iron in his forge and shouting the most terrible obscenities. Susan is simply terrifying…she scared me to death.

"She just sits, staring into space, her eyes seeing nothing.

The other kids are crying their eyes out and, then…then, you see…Norah…Norah…"

The young constable, coughed, and blew his nose violently. His voice started to break up.

Annie forced him to continue. "Go on, Bernard. Tell me about, poor, Norah."

Constable Sheridan turned away to try to get his emotions under control. He, then turned back to Annie, and said hurriedly:

"She hung herself from a rafter in the store-room," he said, quickly turning his head away again.

Annie held her head in her hands and rocked back and forth. She should be there, not here, with strangers: back with real people not with mummers, pretenders, actors… they're not real…

She roused herself. "Bernard, who is with them? They shouldn't be left alone."

"Sergeant Clarkson. He's a very good man and dearly loved poor Norah."

Annie stood up, her voice now back under her control. "Thanks, Constable Sheridan. You go to your good Superintendent. I'll just finish up this matter and then I'm going home."

"Grandmother, the Superintendent said whenever you wanted to go home, I was to drive you there immediately."

Annie nodded her thanks and went to where the police doctor was bending over the body of Polonius.

***

Meanwhile the sensible, local constable had brought the Australian Theatre Manager of the 'Elizabethan', down and introduced him to Superintendent Manders, in a loud voice. He waved to Annie, who hurried down to join him.

"Thank you. Constable le Breton." She turned, so that Manders could hear the reply of the young constable. "Did you find out which hotel the cast is staying at?"

"Yes, it's the Regent Hotel, near Newtown station, Madam. It's a good hotel, safe and secure. The Management here uses it whenever it has a touring company visiting Australia. It's not five stars, but it is a very close imitation of one. I've arranged for police to guard all entries and exits and instructed them to get a list of all hotel employees, including the cleaners".

"Well done, Constable. Oh, I see, the Super has gone to talk to your Inspector. I'll join them."

As Annie came to Superintendent Manders, she heard him speaking to the local Inspector.

"I've looked at the corpse of Polonius, Inspector. I'm certainly not a doctor, but I'll bet it's poison. But possibly a poison that takes a while to take effect."

Annie broke into the conversation. "That's interesting Super. If Angela's death is the result of poison, which I think it will be, then why did it take so long to take effect. I think it's quite possible she was dead when she was shown to us, in the audience, as lying dead, 'where…

Manders finished the quotation: "'*there is a willow grows aslant a stream…*'. Yes, I understand, but that raises questions, doesn't it? The stagehands who put her in the pretend stream and took her out, would have been required to have known that. Would so many be complicit in the scheme? Could she have been still alive in the stream? Dying without a doubt, but still alive?"

"That is far more likely," Annie agreed. "Let's grab the stagehand, or hands, now and ask them: it could cut the work in half."

"Good idea. I'll do it." He lifted up his powerful voice: "The stagehands who handled Ophelia as she was placed into the stream, come down to me here…immediately." There was frantic whispering on stage, then a tall, strong, young man wearing work clothes, vaulted over the edge of the stage and stood in front of Manders - whose body actually hid that of Annie's, who grabbed this chance to sit down in the front row of the stalls. She had, of course, met with Charlie previously when she investigated the 'rubbish issue'.

The stagehand faced the Superintendent.

"I'm Charlie Wilks, sir. I did it on my own. There were supposed to be two of us, but Jeremy had a touch of the runs - something he'd drunk, he thought - sir, and I told him I could do it; she only weighed as much as a child. I followed the cues, and right on cue, I went to the imitation stream and Angela was standing waiting. I lifted her up; I think she was very tired, as she didn't speak, while her head fell back against my shoulder. She had given a glorious performance and I thought she was just 'done in,' and was glad it was over. She breathed out quite forcibly in a very strange way.

"That scene requires split second timing, sir, so I couldn't stand there, gaping any longer; I only just jumped out of the frame a nanosecond before the lights hit the body."

Charlie was not dumb. "I see what you're getting at, Sir. You think she was dying, don't you?"

"It's a possibility I have to consider, Charlie. I thought she could even be dead."

"No way, sir! Definitely, no way! She had such beautiful eyes; they were moving back and forth, back and forth. Could she have been sick? …Very likely. I never thought of that; the breathing was very strange, loud, not regular - you know what I mean. When I got back to Jeremy, he asked me how it went, and I said to him: 'I think the poor kid's utterly exhausted; she looks on her last legs…'

"Blimey! That's sounds rough, doesn't it? I didn't mean it like that. All of us would do anything for that actress, not like the other bloody, snotty-nosed daughter of Polonius, the real Ophelia. She was a bastard, that one, beggin' your pardon sir".

"Thank you, Charlie Wilks, you have been very helpful. One last question. Who hated the girl so much they have killed her?"

The man looked stricken. "I don't know how to answer that, sir," and to his great embarrassment, his face began to crumple, and he began to cry like a child. He turned his head away from the policeman and struggled to get himself back in control.

He blew his nose very loudly, then turned to face Manders. "Sir, it sounds corny I know, but I've been in 'show business,' a few years now, and I've become used to the petty feuds, the jealousy, the fact that many actors are just horrible people, who seem to like nothing better than to show up other actors or, to ruin their entrances, or their lines or, they manoeuvre themselves so that they get a better share of the stage lights. I've seen all their tricks. But I've also seen their unbelievable kindness, and their attempts to help each other, as well, when there are real emergencies.

"Actors are funny people, sir. I hate them, and I love them. I know that sounds daft. But with this girl Angela, who joined us - from an amateur acting studio - only when the usual Ophelia became ill – *or so she said*. I didn't believe a word of it. I think she fudged the illness in order to see the amateur understudy, Angela, make a gigantic mess of the part...and why? Because Angela was everything that the Honourable Annabelle was not. She was truly beautiful, and most of all, she was a virgin...in fact, she was every-thing that she, Annabelle was NOT."

"You weren't here, sir, when the elderly woman police expert - that, 'Watson' woman - when she showed Annabella up for what she was. She saw straight through the phoney Annabelle. Boy, we loved that – all of us. She wiped the floor with that revolting slut who was left livid with fury."

The 'elderly' woman police expert thought it was about time she made herself visible. She rose from her seat, behind Manders. The stagehand gasped, his hand to his mouth. "Blimey, Missus, I didn't mean to be so rude … I apolo-gize..." Annie held up her hand.

"Why should you apologize, Charlie? I think you are one of the most perceptive people on the stage tonight...." She smiled, "you were completely correct, I am an 'old woman'. But I have a question that I want to ask you."

"Ask away, mam. If I know it, I'll answer honestly. If I don't, I'll tell you, I don't."

"Before the actors go on, each night, is it customary to have a little drink, a sip of … say, a tiny bit of alcohol… or something to help the voice?"

"No, nothing alcoholic, but yes, they do have a little drink of some beverage. It is a recommended Health Food drink for cleansing the throat. Not only the actors, but the stagehands as well. That makes sense; you don't want the invisible men – that the audience never see – start coughing and clearing their throats when they are changing a scene, or performing some, 'unpleasant to see', task. I don't take anything, but my friend Jeremy does…"

"The man who had a gastric attack tonight," Annie queried.

"That's right."

"Tell me, did he have any vomiting before the gastric attack?" Charles put his fingers to his lips and whispered: "Missus, please speak softly. He could be sacked if he was thought to be ill. Yes, he did have a short burst of vomiting and I told him it served him right for drinking that stupid drink."

"I see, did Polonius also drink the tonic, Charley?"

"Always. He was very keen on Natural Medicines. I'm not".

"What about Angela? She wouldn't have known about the usual drink, would she Charlie?"

"I think she did know, or at least, I saw Polonius explaining the tradition, to her. She was such a naïve, innocent girl, that she would have accepted his advice as gospel. I saw her drinking from his brew, a small amount, but she did drink."

"Thank you, Charlie. I think Jeremy was the lucky one. Unless the Superintendent wants you, you may return to the stage."

Manders waved his hand dismissing Charlie Wilks, then turned to Annie. "Now, what the hell is this about the drink? Why is that important? Yes, I know, you have probably traced the origin of the poison", he grinned, "but, so what...?"

"Remember your chemistry, Superintendent. Cyanide, if given by mouth, produces sharp convulsions of pain, then vomiting and then diarrhea, in that order.

"Death will follow quickly, if the dosage is large, then much slower if the dosage is smaller, or not at all, if only a sip is taken. Could I suggest, Superintendent, that a search be made for the bottle, or glasses, used. The two young Constables could do that quickly, starting, of course in the dressing room of Polonius."

Manders stood, staring at Annie. "You're serious about this, Mrs Watson?"

"Never been more so."

"All right!" He raised his voice. "Constable Sheridan and Constable le Breton, come to me instantly."

After speaking to the Superintendent, the two constables were instructed to go to Annie. She spoke quietly. "Listen, you know about the Health Food Drink?"

They said they did. Annie then informed them she wanted them to find the bottle, or the glass used.

"Don't bother wasting your time looking in the usual places to look for rubbish, such as wastepaper bins etc, but look in places you would never, normally, hide anything." She noticed their bewilderment. "I mean look among bone fide medicines, that is, real medicines, or with underclothing. Look especially, under *dirty underclothing*; underneath vomit, that might be in a chamber pot, or similar vessel…" She noticed the repulsed faces that both men were pulling.

"Don't worry, hot water and a nail brush, will get rid of everything. Now, off you go and let me know the result."

Constable le Breton asked: "Does this mean that the poison was put there by Polonius, and he is the murderer?"

Annie laughed. "Oh, if it were all that simple, Constable! Not in a million years. He was a victim, nothing else. Off you go! One thing we can be sure of in this crazy and horrible murder, is that the person in whose dressing room the poison is found, will be the last person of all the cast, to have committed the crimes. Now, off you go! And hurry up! I want to go home."

***

It was approaching 2.00am when two dirty and slightly smelly, young constables, came back to the two Superintendents and the lesser police who were sitting close together exchanging notes.

They came to Superintendent Manders. "Sir, we found

the bottle which we think is the poison bottle. We found it in Polonius's room after searching all the others. It was hidden in a filthy place, but the actress who plays the part of Gertrude, said it was Polonius's Health Food drink, which he gave many members of the cast before they went on…
…including Angela Cerney."

With a pair of prongs, which they explained they had found in the props room, they carefully opened a small cardboard box, showed the contents to the Superintendent and then they closed it hurriedly.

Manders had taken a quick sniff of the contents and made a horrible face. "Well, that's certainly no Health Food Drink. It stinks!"

Constable le Breton, with a perfectly straight face, said, "No, it certainly is not a Health Food Drink, sir, that's the smell of very strong urine; we're of the opinion it is male urine. We found it in a receptable that would only be appropriate for a male."

Manders snapped at his constable. "You, Sheridan, take hold of that and we'll send that to our own special police surgeon; he'll move heaven before he'll give up on a task as difficult as this. I think the surgeon attached to this area is a sham, a joke, nothing less." The Constables moved away, as Bob Peters came to his, one time, Inspector.

He spoke wearily. "Super, I can't last out much longer. Do you think we can do anymore tonight? I don't honestly think we can. Everyone is absolutely worn out and drained, not only with the big production, but with the shock and emotion.

"Could we arrange for some large police vans – those vans that hold about 12 passengers and get this crowd back to their hotel. They'd be under surveillance there, and we could take up the job tomorrow, say at about 10.00am. What do you think?"

"You are the epitome of common sense, Superintendent". He turned to his sergeant. "Inspector Watkins, arrange the police vans, refuse to take 'no' for an answer: remind them there are two Superintendents here, *and they demand it.* Inspector Scully, you and Constable le Breton, get this crowd into the vans and, you, Sheridan, you drive superintendent Peters and Mrs Watson home…quick smart now!"

It was all accomplished in just under 30 minutes, even with the Theatre Manager insisting on hanging a very large home-made sign inside the front glass doors, which stated:

'The Theatre is closed; it has now gone Dark.'

Peters began to doze off in the car. Annie was determined to keep him awake until he reached his home. She deliberately shifted and squirmed in her seat and bumped into the elderly man, each time, she thought he was ready to fall asleep.

They were mainly silent; the only time Annie spoke was when they had stopped in front of Peters' house – which he had bought after the dearly loved, old Constable Potts died. It was opposite Annie's house, and the old sandstone cottage, had a very important place in the history of the village of Bexford North.

"Now, Bob, have you your house key ready? Right. Now, I'll call you, on the phone, about 9.00am. I shall get over to

Reg and Susan now and we'll go back to the house of horrors tomorrow morning, about 9.30am. OK?" Peters mumbled a reply.

Without bothering to comment, Constable Sheridan jumped from the car, and taking the arm of the elderly Superintendent, led him to his front door and actually opened, the door with the key, which Peters held out to him.

The young man patted the shoulder of his senior officer and ran back to Annie in the car.

"Grandmother, do you want to get out here, or do you want me to drive you to Reg and Susan's house?"

"You are your mother's son, Bernard. You can read my mind. Take me there, would you, please. You could drive up the side driveway to the back door; I see the lights are all still on."

The constable nodded and slowly drove up the drive to the Cerney's back door. He helped his beloved grandmother out of the car, and, only when she demanded it, did he leave her and return to the police station; he would then be free to go home to bed.

It was close to three o'clock in the morning.

***

Annie, praying silently for wisdom, pushed open the back door of the house. She stood still on the threshold, her eyes taking in the whole scope of the tragedy that had hit this family.

Reg Cerney, now grey headed, but still a strong, powerful

wiry man, was sitting in his usual chair before the fire, but there was no fire. Susan, now grey and plump, sat at the table, food untouched before her, not moving, eyes focused on nothing.

The children were clustered around both parents; Ben, the first born-male - a strong, sturdy young man - was standing near his father, letting the father's head fall back onto his chest. Two girls were holding onto their mother's hands and reciting the rosary non- stop, over and over and over.

Norah, the dearly loved 'aunt' they had inherited from Nan Brady, the old Dance Pianist, who had entrusted her precious, mentally retarded daughter, Norah, to these two people whom, she considered, the best people she had ever known - was featured in this room tableau as well.

Her special chair was sitting there in its usual place, empty, except for a home-made sign: "OUR AUNT NORAH" hanging from its frame.

There was a weird deathly silence in the room only broken by the murmur of the prayers. Both Reg and Susan were sitting like two dead people; their eyes fixed on nothing and staring, staring, staring…at … *nothing*.

Annie realised she had to do something noisy and dramatic to break through this stultifying deadness which could easily result in death, or insanity, if it were not shattered. It was risky, she knew, but surely, screaming hysterics, were better than… NOTHING.

She took a deep breath then clapped her hands loudly. Raising her voice, she demanded that Ben tell her, *immediately*, the most wonderful memory he had of his sister, Angela.

Ben looked up startled, looked quickly at his mother and father, then after a small pause, began, in a broken voice, to tell a story of an occasion when they had a picnic down at the creek, and Angela thought she would paddle her feet..."

"...and wouldn't you know, Lady Ann, she slipped into the freezing water..." softly continued Mary the next oldest. She nudged Raymond...who gulped and said... "No, you've got it all wrong, she didn't fall in, Ben pushed her..."

"I did not; you did; you're always clumsy, isn't he, Mum". Susan brought back from the brink, rallied to the defence of her best loved son... "No, he didn't, did he Poppa?"

Reg stirred and shifted his gaze and looked at his family as if he were seeing them for the first time. He struggled to speak...to concentrate on what he was being asked... "Your mum should know; Ben was Angela's favourite."

The big man rose from his chair and rushed to Annie pleading, loudly: "Lady Ann, Lady Ann, Lady Ann...how can we live now... after this?"

She took the giant of a man into her arms, and he began to cry, and cry, and cry. Soon, Susan joined him... then the kids. Annie whispered to Susan: "Make some tea, love, make lots of tea." Susan jumped up and ran to the kitchen. This was something she knew she *could* do.

Annie turned Reg's chair away from the empty fire and had it facing the rest of the family. She spoke hurriedly and softly to Ben.

"Ben, is there any whisky, or strong drink in the house; that's what your poor father needs now."

Ben looked startled but hurried from the room. He

reappeared, bringing back a glass of what looked like cola, but it, of course, was whisky. Reg drank it, without even comprehending it was alcohol. He was never a very strong drinker; very soon the effects began to show.

He began to talk about Angela, and once started, didn't seem able to stop. The rest of the children all chipped in with their stories of their truly loved big sister. Annie heard again the story of her son, now the great Professor William Watson, when a student, once found by Reg, reading in Greek to Angela in her cot when she was a tiny infant, to her father's astonishment, amusement and delight.

The tea was served with whispered suggestions from Annie to the girls, to look for any sweet biscuits, or cakes they had. While they were doing this, she reminded the children that on the morrow, they would need to make many pots of tea for all the village residents who would be coming in droves to offer their condolences, once the news broke with the morning news.

She advised them to get in touch with the elderly German manager of the general store, to see what she might have; to get in touch also with the cake shop as soon as it opened, as well. Both shops would need to know in advance that they could have many people seeking foodstuffs in the next few days. She reminded them the shops were locally owned and it was only fair that they should be warned.

Annie tried to think of all the every-day activities the family could do; this would stop the deadly…nothingness of what she had first seen. She even suggested that Susan whip up another batch of cup-cakes to be prepared for the morrow. Soon half the family was busy in the kitchen.

About 45 minutes after Annie had arrived in that deadly room, it was a buzz of talk and stories and 'remembering'. Then there was silence.

Reg shushed his family. "Lady Ann, thank you. I know what you have done. You have saved us, once again. Now I want something more.

"You and Superintendent Peters were privileged to see our precious and angelic child in her first great role of the innocent girl, Ophelia, in the wonderful play by the great man, Shakespeare." He cleared his throat. "The kids have read it to me, and I do understand the role that she played, and how difficult it was. We were so hoping to see her tonight... but..." his voice trailed off, then started again with a loud gulp. "*Anyhow, you DID see her.* Would you tell all of us what was she like? Were you proud of her? Was the company pleased with her? She was so thrilled at being offered this chance. She said, for an Australian, to be given this chance could only happen in dreams."

Reg took Annie's work- roughened hands, in his, and kissed them. "Tell us, Lady Ann."

Annie sat down in Norah's chair, deliberately. "Now, listen carefully everyone. Tonight, the Cerney family have something to be so proud of, that you will be talking and writing about, for generations to come.

"Let me tell you, Angela, knocked them for six. She was the greatest Ophelia the Theatre Manager had ever seen. Photos of her and her name will live on in books and articles, while great Dramatists of the future will speak of 'The

Australian amateur actress, Angela Cerney, who triumphed over a Royal Shakespearean Company'.

"Not only in her acting, which stunned them, but her behaviour, her modesty, her obvious purity – in fact, the great leading man, who played Hamlet, himself, gave a rave account of her ability and declared her to have been the exact character that Shakespeare intended. Hamlet declared her to be the greatest Ophelia he had ever known.

"As you would know, from your reading, Ophelia goes mad as a result of her love for Hamlet, then his rejection of her; truly her 'mad scenes' left me terrified.

"Superintendent Peters who, as you know, did not have the chance, while growing up, to get to know about our great Literature and our great Dramatists - such as Shakespeare. That is the reason we were there tonight. He wants, in his retirement, to learn all the things he never had the chance, or the wealth, to know before.

"Now, you know me – you've always known me – so you know I did have the great opportunity to do all that, when I was growing up, but, as an adult, I became a very poor woman. So, Bob Peters and I struck a deal. I'd guide him in discovering all our great Literary history; we'd go to every great performance held in Sydney.

"You know all that. I only repeat it, so you will realise why Peters' impression of tonight's performance of Angela, is so important.

"He was 'ENTRANCED' – that was his word. He repeated it a dozen times at least. He couldn't get over it; he couldn't take his eyes from her. He even criticized the leading man and said he wasn't a patch on Angela's understanding and portrayal of the role.

"You might think I'm just making that up. In a few hours when Robert Peters, the poor man, gets some rest – he's had a terrible job with all the police to cope with, and all the tasks he's had to do this night. He was dead on his feet when the police dropped him at his door; he will see you tomorrow and I assure you, he will be raving, as he did last night.

"Reg, Susan, and the entire family. Your precious Angela was only with you for a short time, but while she was here, she gave you the greatest gift she could give to you - in her total love for you."

Reg was the first to recover. "Lady Ann, what went wrong? How did she die?"

"That's difficult to say, at this stage, Reg. However, something you may not know, will help you to understand the way the death came about.

"An actor has to guard one part of his body more than any other part, and that is…" Ben put up his hand. "…yes Ben?"

"I'm guessing, Lady Ann, but as they talk all the time, so that we can understand the story, their voices need to be clear and not muffled, the whole time…"

"You are completely right, Ben. Yes, actors' voices are their main worry and concern. Just image what it would be like if an actor had to deliver a very serious line and he is doubled up with a wracking cough, or has a slight throat infection and speaks as though he has something caught in his throat. He could be 'boo-ed' from the stage.

"Well, so what? You are asking yourselves. Well, actors are ordinary people, and ordinary people often do strange things. Actors have a number of ways in which they cope with this ever-present danger. They gargle a lot, drink special drinks which clear the throat, they suck special lozenges, some even spray certain, dangerous, mild doses of poison into their open mouths, and many even pray, very devoutly, before going on - pray that their voices will 'hold out'.

"One of the actors, who plays Polonius, the father of Ophelia, was a strong 'Health-Food' advocate; he used a special tonic which he offered to other players as well, many of whom actually took a sip, or two, from the bottle he carried with him everywhere.

"Now, Angela was naturally timid, and in awe of these great actors, who had come all the way from England just to be here in Australia, and she was anxious - as all of us would be – not to be seen as an ignoramus, and one who didn't know what you did in the real world of the Theatre. Remember, she only had ever known the rarefied atmosphere of the Acting Studio before last night.

"So, when Polonius asked the new, nervous, 'understudy' if she would like a spoonful of the mixture which she saw other actors taking, she agreed and thanked the kind old man gracefully.

"Unknown to her and to the actors, a dreadful poison had been added to the syrup. She must have only had a small amount, as she then went on the stage, and the poison didn't take effect for such a long time afterwards. The very good stagehand, Charlie Wilks, who put her in the 'stream' declares she was definitely alive then, but he was worried, as she appeared exhausted. The good man thought the youngster was just tired out. He couldn't stop talking about the way she had presented Ophelia: he had never seen the like of it – it was so beautiful."

Annie stood up. "So, it could well be that Angela died through a terrible accident, but it could also mean something quite different. Now" she smiled broadly, "I am no longer a 'spring chicken', so if I don't get to bed soon, I'll end up on your hearth, out to the world.

"Reg, would you lend me your big son, Ben, to take this old woman home?" Ben came immediately to Annie, who then hurried to each one of the family and kissed each one of them. Reg clung to her. He whispered: "I'll never forget what you've done for us, Lady Ann"

Annie hurried out the back door and took the strong brawny arm of the eldest son, Ben. As soon as they were out of hearing, Anne asked. "Ben, who cut Norah down? Which police were there? Did the police surgeon come? Will it be classified as an 'accidental death' or will there have to be an autopsy and a coronial enquiry? Quickly, fill me in. I have to be back to that blasted theatre at 10.00am - and I simply must get some sleep."

Ben Cerney was an intelligent, and sensible, young man.

"I understand perfectly, Lady Ann. Well…Sergeant Clarkson was the only policeman here. He is a very kind and compassionate man. He actually loved Norah and would do anything to protect her. He cut her down, did the preliminary examination, arranged for the body to be taken away to the morgue, and had the police surgeon sign all the necessary certificates, that are needed. He's hoping it will be just glossed over as an 'accidental death'. He said that Dad and Mum might not survive an actual court appearance, as the suicide was the result of the greatest tragedy, they had ever experienced in their lives.

"Believe me, Lady Ann, Sergeant Clarkson will do everything he can to avert more suffering. Truly, my parents have suffered enough! The sergeant thought so, too."

They stood at Annie's door, and she had extracted her key from her purse. "Thank you, Ben. Yes, I think the group that Superintendent Manders now has, is the best you could find anywhere. Manders and Watkins, even Clarkson have known Norah for a good part of their lives".

The young man started to unravel. "Oh, dear God! It was so horrible. Lady Ann…helping Clarkson cut her down…" and the good young man burst into scalding tears.

Annie held him tightly, then released him. "Steady goes it, Ben. Try to get your parents to bed. Give Reg another shot of whiskey if you have any, and I suggest you boil some milk and put a shot of whiskey in that for your mum." Ben looked a little shocked at that suggestion but promised to do exactly that.

Annie kissed him lightly on the cheek and opened her door. If she didn't get to bed quickly, she could be in danger. She almost ran to her bedroom undressed quickly and, for the first time in her life, let her clothes fall on the floor, turned on the wall heater and fell into bed. Her son's voice startled her.

"Mum, I know how exhausted you must be…just give me two minutes to pass on some messages and then you can sleep."

Annie listened, her eyes opened wide as she paid close attention to what she was being told, as she changed the waking time on her bedside clock, then gave him an important message for Peters, said, "Good night. Please turn out the light," and fell back on her pillows.

Within two minutes, she was deeply, soundly and dreamlessly asleep.

***

Next morning, punctually at 10.00am Bob Peters came across to Annie's house, carrying the morning papers. There was a note from the professor, her son, on the front door. It asked the caller to go around to his door on the other side of the house, as his mother was not well.

***

Professor William Watson opened his door and quietly welcomed his neighbour inside his small flat. They had known each other for years now, and so were completely at home with each other.

The Professor began speaking before Peters had sat down. "You know what she's like, Robert. She went without any sleep at all last night, had no dinner, and not, as yet, any breakfast. That would weaken anyone, even half her age.

"I took one look at her when she finally fell into bed. She was a wreck. As soon as she was asleep, I crept in and altered her bedside clock; it had been set for 7.00am. I changed it to 11.00am

"I also didn't want her to see the newspapers. I see you have them. I have the serious one, Mum gets. I see you have both the major morning ones: Please, let me see both."

"William, the good delivery chap left last night's papers for me, as well. Look at that Headline:

THEATRE MYSTERY: ACTOR DIES.

Now see what this morning says:

THE HAMLET DEATH. IT'S
MURDER!"

"Now, we're in trouble, son. That explains why the Press are out in such numbers outside Reg and Susan's place, this morning. There was even a television truck there as well… God help us!"

William was equally aware of the difficulties now. "Robert, I know she wanted you to see the Cerney family this morning, but I don't think you can risk it." Peters nodded in agreement.

"Perhaps," Robert Peters said, "later today, I could go around the back way and come in, via the forge itself. I'll cross that bridge later."

He looked at the tall young man, now mercifully strong, and healthy. "But what about your mother? How can we get her back to the rotten crime scene safely. I know full well, there is no point in even suggesting she stay at home."

William laughed. "You and I both know that, so I'm not

even going to try to suggest it. I'll cop enough flak from changing her waking hour on her clock. But with this extra time, I can cook her some breakfast before she returns to the Theatre, which I believe is her intention.

"But before I forget. She had thought of something which she was worried about, and which she was berating herself for forgetting, and asked me, if I saw you, to tell you about it."

"Yes, son. What was it? If your extraordinary mother thought it was important, then it certainly will be."

"She said to remind you that the Acting Studio personnel would, without doubt, have been in the audience somewhere last night, and would have, openly, or surreptitiously, used their movie cameras to record the 'once in a lifetime' experience, of one of their pupils, getting this glorious chance to perform with an illustrious Shakespearean, high class, Company from the UK. They would use this for advertisement to attract pupils.

"Robert, I have no technical knowledge, so I don't even know how those new hand-held 'movie-cameras' work, but everyone's talking about them now." He gave a boyish laugh. "I have trouble with taking photos with my little 'Brownie."

Peters was left with his mouth open at Annie's news. "That is very, very important, William. I'll get onto it as soon as I get to the theatre. What a brilliant idea; it never occurred to me!"

He stood up. "I must get moving. Manders and his team will be wondering why I am not there."

"Just before you go, Robert, did you hear the news on

the commercial radio this morning? Do you know how bad it was?"

"No, I didn't, son. but I saw coming over here, just now, the two constables, Clarkson and Sheridan, standing guard at the street end of the lane by the side of Reg and Susan's house. There was a television truck – as I said - with reporters on the ground, with their mikes, grabbing any local who had the misfortune to pass by. I was attacked by two men and a ferocious woman, but I remained silent except for saying clearly and loudly, again and again: 'No comment; No comment; No comment'.

"That is vile, Robert. Thank God, those two, wonderful constables, are holding the fort. But… wait a minute… dear God! They've had no rest either. Can you arrange a relief for them, Robert?"

"I certainly can. I'll pop across to see them briefly…if I can… and inform them I'll do my best to relieve them, within the hour. Thanks William. " He stood up, grabbed his hat and hurried out through the door.

Professor Watson, the great Classic Scholar, Head of the Classic Department at the famous, old university, and the terror of all advanced students, who complained of the difficulty, of not only learning to *read* Greek, *but of speaking ancient Greek as well*, now went to the kitchen and looked with apprehension at the eggs and the bacon.

To him, speaking numerous ancient tongues was dead easy, cooking was a mystery; it was too difficult, to even begin to comprehend.

An hour later, Annie sat at her breakfast table with the

remains of the burnt eggs and the charred bacon that her son had prepared for her. She had managed to eat the 'burnt offerings,' by averting her eyes from the food altogether, aware of the kindness that had motivated the meal.

She demanded to know if the message had been delivered to the Superintendent... that was, of course, after she had expressed her irritation – in somewhat vigorous terms - to him in making her so desperately late for the meeting with the cast and the police.

She was only placated by his promise to drive her all the way to the theatre, or the Hotel, wherever the police were; and secondly, for letting her know what the radio and the newspapers had to say.

"Is there any chance you can get across there to the family today, Billy?"

"Well, I intend to try, Mum, but I'm not going to give those fiendish hounds any information they have no need of knowing; I'm only marking dissertations today, so I'll stay at home. When I come back here, from my trip to the city with you, the new guards will be on - Peters will fix that, I know; I'll then slip across and go in from the back gardens."

"All right, son. I'm sorry to be so grumpy. Getting old, I think. Can't take sleepless nights anymore." She gave a little laugh. "I'm wearing low heels today; that will help me considerably. If you are talking to your sister, the beautiful, Lady Penelope, you needn't mention I refuse to wear those crippling, fashionable, three-inch heels she bought for me, ever again. Promise?"

"It's a deal, mum. Now, leave the dishes, I'll do them later. Get ready: the sooner you're ready to go, the sooner you will be where you belong … with the police. I'll get the car out now."

Annie wore her hair in a tight bun for this exit and tied a scarf around her head, hoping that she had not appeared in any of the news broadcasts on either television or radio.

She had reached the car, now parked near her front gates, safely and was delighted to see she had been ignored. Her son came running and jumped into the driving seat, just as the red-haired female T.V. journalist spotted him and ran towards them.

Billy Watson blasted the horn at her and turned the car, so close to the reporter, she had to jump out of the way, or she would have been run over. She screamed, and cameras were immediately turned on the driver of the car who, accelerating wildly, raced away.

When they had put several miles between them, and the Press, Billy turned to his mother and said, "Now, remember Mother, if you are ever in such a situation like that, just do as I did, keep utterly calm, and politely ask the journalists if you can assist them…in fact do just what I did, back there!" He started to laugh, helplessly, Annie joining him.

She blew him a kiss and said: "We're both cut from the same bolt of material, I think, Billy."

***

Manders, looking rather pale and drawn, had ordered the

entire cast, including the 'Players', to be transported from the Hotel to the theatre. They were all gathered together in the Green Room. More chairs were brought in from the set and the dressing rooms.

It was a very large room, having been extended twice in its history, so now it could hold a full company with even more persons than they had with 'Hamlet'.

On the table near the door was the latest newspaper with its headline in huge letters:

EXTRA EXTRA EXTRA
ANOTHER MURDER! THIS TIME POLONIUS!
IS THE THEATRE CURSED?

Annie grimaced, then turned to greet both Superintendents, Manders and Peters. They spoke together quietly, and Annie looked shocked. The men then took her to a tall, very thin, lady who was standing, having just arrived as well. Annie noticed the red rims of the eyes and the black clothes. The woman was standing near the table stacked with the evening and morning papers.

Peters did the introduction, "This, Lady Ann, is the Principal of the Acting Academy, where our beloved Angela came from, Ms Agnes Pottermore."

Annie shook the hand swiftly. "You are certainly welcome, Ms Pottermore. Come and sit near me at the table here. These men would have you standing for ever, give them a chance." She took the arm of the tall woman, and they sat close together at the table.

"Ms," Annie began and stopped, as the woman interrupted quietly. "Would you kindly call me by my first name, Agnes?"

"Certainly, Agnes, if you will give me the same token of friendship, and call me, 'Annie.'" She raised her eyebrows and the woman nodded vigorously.

"Agnes did the two Superintendents ask you about a movie camera? I don't have one, but I was thinking of buying one if I could learn how to use it."

"These are good policemen, Annie. How clever of them to think one of us – the teachers on my staff - would be here when our prize student was understudying a great actress in a leading role. *Of course, we were there*, as many of us who could get seats, and we used three cameras to record nearly everything." She looked embarrassed.

"Annie, I didn't think of copyright, or anything other than the fact that, after all our years of trying, we had succeeded at last – we had a student playing a major role in a world-renowned London Company.

"I've been now informed by Mr Cohen that I have broken all the rules and that I must hand over the film, or else he would be forced to bring in the lawyers. I had no option but to hand it over. Truly, Annie, it never occurred to me that I was breaking any laws…"

"Oh, please don't upset yourself any more Agnes. I would have done the same. Why can't you have a copy of your great success? Please leave it to me, I'll see you have a copy: my son in law is a great barrister. I'll ring him this morning…"

"Please, Annie…" Agnes looked around furtively. "Don't worry, I handed over *my copy*, but my second in charge, and the voice coach, still have theirs…" She had to stop as Annie was laughing, helplessly.

"What the authorities don't know won't hurt them, Agnes. I'll hold back on the lawyers, then." She looked up. "Excuse me, Agnes. I'll just speak to the Supers for a moment; I'll come back to you, after that."

Peters had called Annie over, as he and Manders, were being instructed on how to use one of the new movie cameras by the Theatre's electrician. The man had inserted the film into the camera and was experimenting with the size trying to make it as large as he could. He thought, as with the Pictures - or, what they had to call them, now - the Movies… the principle was the same, he was wondering if he could use a big projector with the small film. He thought it was worth a try, anyhow.

They had decided to use what they had, in the meantime. Using a new, snowy-white scene-flat; they tried the camera, and found it gave an image about two feet square. They thought that would do.

They were not going to show the whole play, of course, only those scenes where Ophelia was present. Annie suggested they place Agnes Pottermore in the front row with, Hamlet, Charlie, Jeremy, Claudius, Guildenstern and Constable Le Breton sitting close together, or standing, just behind the front row.

The police quickly re-arranged the room so that the majority – including the 'Players', were at least able to see the relatively small video image. The police huddled together then asked Annie to suggest what they should look for in the film.

Annie spoke clearly and slowly to the assembled people.

"This time we are asking YOU, as the experts that you are, both on the stage, and behind the scenes - to help us. You know this play backwards. We don't. We are only looking on from one side. You know when an actor forgets the ending of a line; you know how to save the actor by changing slightly what YOU say – in other words – you know all the tricks of the trade – and what a glorious trade you have.

"In the front row we have another expert, the incredible teacher who formed Angela into such a perfect Ophelia, Ms Pottermore.

"We want all of you, especially the stagehands, who possibly know the play better than some of the actors taking part – to watch for anything that startles you… or you think: 'wait a minute, that's not right'; if any part of the scenery moves when it shouldn't, if it throws shadows, or if you see anything there, that shouldn't be there, or wasn't there, before, or after, that particular scene…I'm being vague, as we just want to know of anything that is, 'out of place', or causes you a momentary frown, or surprise. That's about as clear as I can make it, Supers. Just one more thing, then I'll get off this scene and leave it to you."

Annie turned her head away for a moment to get her emotions under control. When she turned back again, her face was like flint and her voice cold and incisive. "I need to tell you when I first came here this afternoon, the Superintendent Manders informed me of both the autopsy findings, and the Science Lab had sent the report on the bottle of, so called, 'Health Food' drink.

"First of all: the autopsy report. The forensic experts

found that Angela had died of a large dose of cyanide which she received in that 'innocent' drink. It appears likely that that extraordinary, magnificent, courageous young woman played half the scene when she was in terrible pain. Charlie Wilks remarked, that when he put her in the 'pretend' stream, he thought she was simply exhausted. She was in fact close to death, which actually took place as we were gazing at her, from the stalls."

Annie's voice wobbled; she closed her eyes then forced herself to continue. "The drink when analysed, even in its polluted state, indicated clearly, a very high level of cyanide: enough, they thought, *to kill the entire company*." There was a collective gasp of horror from the company. Annie looked at the audience before her. "I tell you these gruesome things, not just to scare you, but to make you realise the seriousness of what you have faced... ... and, are STILL facing!

"You have a murderer in your midst, and if you value your lives, then you will pay close attention to all the police tell you to do, and to heed whatever they tell you. Of course, it follows, that you will tell them what you know, or what you suspect. The life you might be saving could well be, *your own*. Watch the film; put your hand up if you want the film stopped."

She spoke sharply to the police: "Run the film".

Annie still had excellent eyesight and stood back from the front, but from where she could see the small screen. There was sudden silence as all eyes were fixed on the screen.

Five hands suddenly were raised at the same time. "Stop the film," ordered Annie. She searched among the raised hands. "Yes, Gertrude?"

The woman lifted a wearied, and pain-etched, face. "Mam, it's that shadow seen behind the large flat." All the other voices agreed noisily. "Yes, that's what it is. Who is it?" Annie looked quickly again at the group. "Charlie Wilks, who was it? You must know."

The young man was worried. He didn't know whether to admit his knowledge, or not. He took one look at the woman - this criminologist - and knew she wouldn't stand for any unnecessary delay. He looked at Annie and said softly, "I think – I could be utterly wrong; it's not easy to tell just from a shadow – but I think it is Rosencrantz." He turned his head round further, "Sorry, sir".

Annie addressed the cast. "If it is Rosencrantz, and he's in the wrong place, where should he be?" There was no reply. She turned to the lead man. "Hamlet, where should he be"

The star raised his head and looked at Annie. "He should be on the other side of the stage – stage right - he's on stage left."

Annie kept her eyes on the white-faced actor and asked icily. "What were you doing on stage left, at that moment?"

Rosencrantz went to speak and struggled to get his voice to work. He suddenly leapt to his feet and ran for his life. Constables - unknown to Annie - jumped up and raced after the actor. The rest of the cast remained still, and silent, until they heard the loud scream of terror that announced the capture, then the shout of triumph as the man was bound and marched back to the crowd of his peers. He seemed more embarrassed, then afraid.

He was struggling uselessly in the policemen's arms and when he eventually was dumped down on a chair. Annie regarded him with interest. She noticed, for the first time, his age; he was much younger than any other of the cast; she saw the weak chin, the real terror that possessed the actor. She softened her tone; this man was no murderer.

"You are a foolish man. Your behaviour has brought you into serious question now, by your foolish attempt to run away. Where were you running to, you silly chap? You are 12,000 miles from home here. There is nowhere to run. Just tell me the truth and, if it has nothing to do with the murders, then you are free."

The man was close to tears. "Could I please write it down, mam? I promise you; it has nothing whatsoever to do with the deaths here. On my oath, I promise you that."

"Well, we don't usually do bargains like that, my boy, but yes, write it down and we'll consider it carefully. If it is, as you say, then we'll certainly keep our part of the bargain." She handed him the notepad, that Peters passed to her.

There was silence as the young man, William Smithers, wrote a short paragraph. He, red-faced with embarrassment, handed it back to Annie and she read it with her eyebrows raised.

"I see. Thank you, Mr Smithers. And a warning. Don't waste our time with such rubbish as that, ever again, or you will be guilty of a serious charge of impeding the work of the police in the pursuit of a killer who has committed serious crimes. Return to your seat immediately."

Annie spoke to Peters and Manders, for a few minutes, then agreed that they should finish the film. She asked for, and received, permission to keep the evidence in the notebook.

Annie watched, with great personal heartache, the rest of the film trying so hard to remove herself from all emotion and fix her attention on the film itself.

She knew however, she was failing to do, as she should. She also observed another phenomenon, which she realised she should have expected: the actors were only absorbed in the film when it depicted them, personally. They were basically uninterested in anyone's else's part.

The same conclusion had been experienced by Peters and Manders. The police came to Annie, and they were soon huddled together, speaking in very soft voices, as to the next move they should take.

Annie apologized. She had really thought they were on a winner - with the movie camera. The others agreed it was a very sensible, sound suggestion, and they had all gained from seeing it. They reminded her that the majority of the police present, had never even seen the play.

They were interrupted by the Theatre Manager who brought in the latest daily papers: There were three:

THEATRE UNDER INVESTIGATION

QUESTIONS ASKED IN PARLIAMENT

WHO WILL BE NEXT? POLICE SUGGEST MURDERS

FOLLOWING THE DEATHS IN TRAGIC PLAY

The papers were placed on the table and largely ignored.

***

Annie sat with both superintendents and the senior police to discuss the whole situation. Annie spoke strongly on the necessity of making sure they all knew the play itself. She was convinced that these murders were following those in Shakespeare's play – in the sequence in which they occurred. In her opinion one of the newspaper headlines was right.

Both Peters and Manders thought that was an interesting angle, but far-fetched, and they should pursue it along with any others they had. It was the only one, at the moment, pointing anywhere, but there could be many others. Or, warned Manders, they could be dealing with a pathological killer who had no sense of right, or wrong, at all.

"Well," Annie stated, "As you are not keen on my slant, as to the motivation in this situation, what about the main motivations when dealing with anything to do with actors?"

"I have to admit, Mrs Watson," said Manders, "I've never had a case with actors before. Have you Robert?"

Peters, tried to remember. "I can't think of any either, son…but it's possible I did. Sorry, I don't think I have any experience in this field at all."

Annie laughed gently. "Well, if two well-known experts in homicide – with umpteen years of experience - say that, then I can only add that the Theatre is the safest place to put your sons and daughters." The others laughed. "Look, let me explain for a moment, what I mean, gentlemen."

"In any stage show, there are gradients of importance. Even in Pantomime, there is a title of '*Principal* Boy', or the 'Fairy *Queen*'. Right?" They nodded. "OK, well what if you had rehearsed, and rehearsed, to get the principal part and another lad, or girl, gets it. What does the 'second best' feel? Joy? No, he feels ANGRY; he could be consumed with ENVY and, if he were a child, he, or she, would probably sulk and hide in his, or her, room.

"Now take that into adult theatre, where not only fame, but also, *FORTUNE* depends on the winning of the 'Star Role', the 'Principal part' – then you could be so consumed with jealousy and anger, you are ready to kill in your rage. Particularly, I would think, if you had worked ten times harder than the one, who was actually given the role."

"But," objected Manders, "if you killed your rival in the adult theatre, you would be destroying the whole production, and no one would get a part. It would be a case of shooting the hen that lays the golden egg."

"That is perfectly true, Super. But think of the average domestic murder. The husband kills his wife, so that no one else could have her; he thus destroys the one thing on earth he loves, or who cared for him. He is left with nothing at all. Or the wife, seeking the freedom to do what she wants to do, shoots her husband, and in doing so, deprives herself of the chance to do anything, but look at cell walls, for the rest of her life."

She smiled at the two senior men. "Well, that's what I'm going to pursue, anyhow. I could be hopelessly wrong, but at least it offers a believable motive. And believe it or not, I do recognize the fact that I'm a mere amateur in this matter. You both have handled dozens of murderers in your careers." She looked around the group. "You'll be pleased to know I've finished talking now." She laughed and pushed her chair back.

Both Superintendents agreed that the only way to find out the truth was by personal interviews. Annie was happy to second that. They decided to split the cast, into groups, including the Players, together with stagehands.

When each Leader had finished his, or her, questions, the Leader would pass onto the next group. It was hoped, in that way, they would cover all the basic questions they needed to ask, and by seeing the police more than once, what one of the police Leaders failed to extract, the next Leader might discover.

Manders quickly divided the whole cast on the stage into four groups. He then indicated the areas they would now move to, either on the stage, itself, or in the stalls area in the space between the seats of the front stalls, and the stage. By grouping all the cast as one, actors were mixed with the two stagehands, and police constables, so each group would have a mixture of both.

Annie noted that the Players were nervous, and apprehensive, at being split up and placed in different groups. She was counting on hearing some original questions from them.

Annie found herself as leader of a group which comprised, Gertrude, Claudius, Horatio, Margaret York and

Charlie Wilks. They sat facing her in the front row of the stalls. Constable le Breton who was assigned to her, sat close to Annie.

Annie let her eyes wander over her group. She decided to start on Gertrude.

"I shall call all of you by your stage names, and the Players and stagehands I know, by their first names…" She looked closely at the middle-aged woman who had such an important role.

"Gertrude, we are intruding on your own personal grief in the death of Polonius. Please bear with us; we are not machines; we are personally, grievously upset, by the death of the young girl, Angela. But regardless of that, there is such a thing as justice and someone here has got away…so they think…with a vile crime, not once, but twice, and we don't know if it is now over, or not.

"We are doing our best to protect you with a multitude of police but, they didn't prevent Polonius death, did they?"

Charlie protested: "But they tried, mam, they tried. That's all we ever can do." Annie looked at the man, her eyes searching for irony, or deceit. She turned to Claudius (Denis le Clerc) but the constable forestalled her, by speaking to the actor first, himself.

"Claudius, you have been very quiet in all the questioning, so far, by the police. What do you think happened? How did Angela die?"

The actor raised his very handsome head. "Well, I can answer that. Angela died because she was a young woman of some looks, but no brains at all, and was so stupid as to fall for Polonius' spurious drinks. He was such an old fool that to receive anything from him, was signing your own death certificate."

Annie forced herself to keep her face blank; she spoke quickly before the constable could collect his thoughts. "An interesting answer. What do you think of that answer, Gertrude? Charlie? Horatio? Margaret? You first, Gertrude." Annie noticed that the woman was trembling.

"Firstly, let me say I am appalled by such speech. And I wonder just why you, le Clerc, would go out of your way to insult the memory of an innocent young girl, and a very decent elderly man."

Claudius smiled his very cruel smile. "I expected an outburst from Polonius', 'bride to be'. We all knew of your affair with a man who was old enough to be your father. It was disgusting. As for the girl: she was a colonial subject of Great Britain, what would you expect of such rubbish."

Stagehand Charlie, stood up, his face red with anger.

"Why you, filthy, little, sissy man. We all know who poor Rosencrantz was running off to, when his shadow was caught by the camera. You've made him your 'toy boy', haven't you? We all know that. And, secondly, I happen to know that all your high-falutin' claims… with your false name, and equally false, background… are all baloney! A descendant from a French count in the 18th century? Don't make me laugh! You are the son of a grease monkey in a car repair shop." He laughed at the actor and went to spit on him.

Constable le Breton quickly moved in – this was something he was familiar with. Annie spoke quickly to defuse the situation.

"That is very interesting, I've made a note of your remarks, Charlie. I'll come back to you in a moment. I just want Horatio's take on Claudius' statement." Annie turned slightly so that she was facing, Horatio.

Annie was uncertain how to approach Horatio. He said he was a friend of the actor, not just as the play dictates, but in real life. Perhaps she should concentrate on that. However, she wanted his reaction to Claudius first.

"Now, Horatio, we have heard Gertrude and Charlie's comments on Claudius' statement. What did you think of it?"

"Why don't you ask the pretty boy, Hamlet. He was the one who raved on about the great Angela, the Ophelia."

"You didn't like her? Did you think her work was too amateurish for your august British company? Or did you simply dislike her, Horatio, as she was an Australian, and not from Britain?"

The actor laughed outright. "I think the only fame she achieved was by her dying. She would have passed into oblivion, had she not died on her first night." He started to giggle. "That's really funny, isn't it? I've heard of First Night nerves, but I think this amateur has scored a new award for having the good sense to die on the first night of her performing, on a real stage, with real actors." He actually laughed at his macabre joke.

"Thank you for being honest with me, Horatio. Now, one more little thing and I'm finished." She shifted in her chair.

"Horatio, you have known Hamlet, or Andrew Hammond-Oates before, I understand."

"Indeed, you asked me that before: do you doubt this for some reason?"

"Not really, Malcolm; I just like to be sure. Did you meet him as a child?"

Horatio was irritated at the harping on this one point. He shuffled his feet and yawned in his boredom. "As a matter of fact, I did. We were at the same acting studio together as youngsters." He looked, with a degree of contempt at the Policewoman. "Why don't you ask me questions about the deaths? Isn't that what we are supposed to be wasting our time on?"

"So, Horatio, you consider it a waste of time to try to determine the individuals behind the deaths of Angela and Polonius?"

"No, I can see that that would interest some people; it just doesn't interest me, that's all."

"Good! Well, that makes it clearer for me. Tell me do you like your work?"

"*Like my work*? What a strange question! Whoever called the vocation of a great actor, *work*? It is a joy - a sensual joy. I feel I can fly after I have been on the stage, in whatever part, for even a small role. I feel as if I am on Mt Olympus with the gods. "

"Do you ever smoke cannabis, Malcolm?"

"That's a strange switch! *How dare you*! To make such a suggestion as that…I'll…"

"Just a moment, son. I was going to say, if you do, it is

advisable to chew some sweet lozenges; they help to hide the smell; many people find it offensive."

Annie turned to Margaret who had begun to speak. "Wait a minute, Margaret... I'll just turn over a page. Right! Now, let's hear your comment."

"I am shocked and, indeed, horrified to hear Horatio has such a vulgar and rude opinion of the very people who help him to earn his salary. I'm not at all surprised to detect the smell of cannabis coming from that man. I'm glad now, I was never forced to know him."

"Thank you, Margaret for your honest opinion

"Now back to Charlie. I haven't forgotten. I have noted what you commented on Claudius' statement. Now while, I still have the chance of talking to you, I want you, Charlie Wilks to tell me what you, yourself, think happened, first to 'Angela as Ophelia'- and then, Polonius."

Charlie closed his eyes, then opened them and spoke slowly. "I simply don't know, mam. If it were only Ophelia's death, it could be put down to a simple error, and the whole thing a tragic mistake. But with Polonius's death following, as well, I don't know where we are.

"If Polonius had Angela's death before him, and the drink was suspected, why wouldn't he just pour out the tonic from the bottle in case it had been polluted in some way, but he didn't. He seems to have died from the same cause as Angela, with the same agonies in dying, and the same awful diarrhea, after he had died. Truly, as you Aussies say: 'It beats me, mate.'"

Annie nodded to the stagehand. "You have just about

summed up the whole thing for us, Charlie. Thank you."

Annie went to get up, when she noticed that Gertrude was making tentative attempts to speak. "Is there something else you'd like to say, Gertrude?"

"Mrs Watson, you are a sensitive woman. If a man were taking this session, I would not say this, but I don't think you would laugh at me."

"I promise all of you, I will not laugh at anyone who helps us to get at the truth, Gertrude. Go ahead."

"I'm fully aware of neurotic women my age, who always see things, that no one else ever sees, or feels things that no one else ever does, but I was reluctant to come to Australia with this show, much as I wanted to see your astonishing country. I felt it was dangerous to come, and once here, that feeling grew and grew on me. Polonius, strange to say, felt the same…"

Annie spoke gently to the actress. "Gertrude, could you be a little more specific…any person? Or is it the play, itself? Ask yourself, did this sensation stem from an actor, the country…whatever?"

Gertrude began to tremble even more, and her beautiful voice started to fall apart. "No, Mrs Watson, all I can say is that it is like a sense of brooding evil hovering over this play, this theatre, this company, and these actors, and… myself." She raised a tear-streaked face. "I think… I shall soon be joining Polonius."

The constable was uncomfortable; he looked to Annie for guidance. She was brisk, and said, firmly. "In that case, the police had better work faster to get this whole sorry mess cleaned up, so we can all rest properly to get over it.

"Thank you, Gertrude, for sharing that with us. It is never easy to speak of personal feelings, or beliefs. You have spoken from the heart; I respect that." She stood up. "They have signalled to me; it's time to change to another group. Just stay where you are; the constable and I will move on to our next group. Thank you."

As they moved away the constable went to speak. Annie shushed him quickly and pretended to look at the list in her hand. "Now, we will have in our next group: Guildenstern – Albert Fellows- Ophelia - the Company one – Richard from the Players, and the Ghost himself, who I must re-member, is Dominic Oddfellow. And there is a stagehand, Jeremy. Charlie spoke of him, they're friends, I think.

"Quickly, tell me, Constable, what did you think of that outburst by Claudius?"

"I was just embarrassed to tell the truth, Mrs Watson. All that homosexual stuff, then the cruel words about the young girl, then the poor elderly actor. Young le Clerc has to become an old actor himself, one of these days."

"And Horatio?"

"Why was he so ready to take offence? Did you smell what I did, as well?"

"I certainly did. I had to hide a smile there, Constable. He talked about Mt Olympus. I think he is floating so high, now, he could probably reach it very soon.

"If you can manage it; and don't say who suggested it, could you happen to have a little peek into his shaving cabinet in his dressing room, and see if you can find any reefers there. Only, of course," she smiled, "if you promise you won't take one, yourself." They both laughed.

"I think I remember which is his dressing room. If the coast is clear I'll get it back to you, as quickly as I can." He smiled broadly. "I promise not to take one."

"Duly noted. Well, remember you are on duty: don't forget that, or they'll never forgive me, if things go wrong. You can go when we finish the next one.

"Now, we've had our comedy, here's the serious stuff."

Annie looked at the young policeman closely; she was truly interested in his reply.

"Now, Constable le Breton, the sensations felt by Gertrude about the whole play, and about this company? What was your reaction to all that, Constable?"

"A load of tripe, if you truly want to know. I don't go much into all that 'feeling stuff'. Ten to one, it's all imagination and caused by an empty belly."

Annie was so surprised, she laughed aloud.

"Ssh! Here we are! Be careful this is a difficult group. I want you to concentrate on Ophelia and Guildenstern. I want to tackle the Ghost; I'll keep Richard the main Player with me." Then unaware of the anticlimax, she added, "When we finish, remind me to get that hotel to provide afternoon tea for the whole cast AND the police…and here we are!

"Good afternoon, everybody." She smiled at the new group, as she settled down and continued. "Now you'll most probably find we are going to ask the same questions which have been asked before, but the sooner we are finished, the sooner we can all get a cup of tea and something to eat."

The actors sat down again and looked at their new Leader. Annie spoke first. "I want to shift us a little way apart for a while. Jeremy, you and Richard, stay with me and the Ghost… If the rest of you would leave a couple of seats vacant, then Constable le Breton will speak to Guildenstern and Ophelia."

Annie and Jeremy looked at the older actors, Dominic and Richard. The Ghost was a fine-looking man, venerable now, with no make-up. She thought he was everyman's concept of a good, aging, clergyman. In fact, both actors were very similar in looks.

"Now, Mr Oddfellow…what? … Your first name? Certainly, if you wish," she smiled at the elderly actor. "Now, *Dominic*, first of all I want to say how much I admired your performance. The role of 'the Ghost' is the most difficult part of all to play in this great tragedy, I think. I have to admit that I've wanted to giggle a bit, at some performances I've seen of 'the Ghost', in the past, but your performance actually had me really scared; it was so convincing. There was a distinctly 'other worldly', or 'spiritual', atmosphere you created, that jolted me, I can tell you"

"That's very kind of you, Madam; it usually is overlooked entirely in the crits, as it's such a small part actually."

Annie lowered her voice. "And that's the reason I wanted to speak to you separately, sir. You spend most of the play just waiting to 'go on'. You must find it boring. What do you do to fill in the time?

Mr Oddfellow was a little embarrassed. "Madam, I write critiques of the actors performing with me. They are never vindictive, and the actors usually ask me, how they 'went' when they come off some difficult scene, or speech."

"I think that's wonderful. It means you know where everyone is, and if anyone's missing from where they should be, you would know of it, wouldn't you?" the man nodded. Annie continued. "Then, if one were missing, you would know. Casting your mind back to last night, can you remember anyone not being where you expected them to be?"

"It's strange you are asking me that. Yes, I did. There was a lot of unusual movement last night. I don't know why. It could have been that we were using an amateur actress who had never before performed in a famous company performance: there could have been a kind of nervousness in the company…you know…expecting everything to go wrong, and then wondering what would happen… and so on."

"In particular, Dominic, any scene that stands out in your mind?"

"I think the worst time was just after Hamlet's first encounter with the ghost. He usually goes stage right and waits, as he is soon back on stage again…he was due to go on, and I couldn't see him anywhere…"

"You are saying that you thought 'Hamlet' was missing? And was he?"

Jeremy broke into the conversation. "Yes, I noticed that, too. I looked up at the flies to see if anything had gone wrong. I also thought…"

"Thought what, Jeremy?"

"That the precious, beautiful, boy-actor, whom the girls

drool over, and everybody adores, had nipped off for a smoke."

There was dead silence. Annie was puzzled at the bitterness and bitchy-ness of the tone. This was odd. "You mean to tell me that he is ruining that glorious voice, by smoking?"

Jeremy grinned: his glee apparent. "Well, he won't have that velvet voice much longer. My old man is a fierce smoker; his voice is horrible."

Richard spoke, strongly outraged, at what had been said. "That's a dreadful slur to cast against one of the greatest actors of the century. His voice is magnificent! I know, for a fact, he doesn't smoke at all."

Anne switched back to Dominic, aware of the enmity between the stagehand and the lead actor, storing away that tiny scrap of information.

"So, Dominic, Hamlet was absent…?"

"Only for about a minute, but you realise that a minute is a very long time to wait for an actor to come on to a bare stage. When he did get there, he was slightly breathless. He has such a beautiful voice: I envy him that greatly: his speech is perfection.

"Naturally, as he is the lead, the star of the show, everyone's eyes are on the Hamlet of the performance; he was more worried about the new amateur, Ophelia, than anyone else. Of course, he would be, he had more to lose, than anyone else." The elderly man frowned vexedly. "No! That's not fair – that sounded bitchy.

"Young Hamlet is a fine and very decent, young man

and I do truly believe he was genuinely concerned for the young girl, Angela.

"Dominic, do you know if he spoke to another actor, before he went on: I mean, *unexpected* speech. You would know what he *should* be saying, did he say anything that struck you as odd?"

"No, I didn't see him talking to anyone else, or hear any unscripted words."

"Thank you, Dominic. Only two more questions: do you have some Health Food drink before you go on, or not?"

"Not on your life. I'm too old to be bothered with all that junk. I simply gargle with salt as I leave the hotel; I've done that all my life; I'm not into health food fads."

"Right, that's a straight answer. Now the last one. Could I ask you for your opinion of your UK Company Manager, Mr George Aspinall?"

The old actor, sorted in disgust. "He's a weak, lily-livered, bastard, who runs away as soon as there is a problem, a big one like this one, or even a little one. This Australian, 'Elizabethan Theatre Manager', Mr James Cohen, is a real manager; he has remained here ever since the tragedy occurred to that glorious young, child, Angela. Thank God, we were informed that another representative of the Firm, that owns the company, is on his way, by plane, to us here. He should be here fairly soon. A good thing too; we won't feel so abandoned then."

Annie shook hands with the actor and asked him to return to the stage and she, Richard and Jeremy, went to Ophelia and Guildenstern who were with Constable le Breton.

"Forgive me for leaving you until last. Now, only a couple of questions and then we hope we can have afternoon tea." She smiled, gently, at Ophelia. "I'm truly sorry, Annabelle, for the death of your good father. He was a good man and a fine actor. I thought his performance of Polonius, the best I have ever seen." The young woman raised a tear-stained face.

"I'm sorry, mam, for my rudeness earlier, and thank you for those words about my father. It's not very sophisticated of me, to say, I adored my father, but I did. I only became an Elizabethan actress because he wanted me to; I wanted to be an actress, but not in roles about people who lived centuries ago."

"That's honest and I appreciate that. Now I've only a couple of questions to ask you and then Jeremy and Richard could have a couple.

"Firstly, did you like the amateur brought in your place?"

"No, I didn't."

"Any reason in particular?"

"I thought she could ruin the show. I thought, as a 'colonial', she would not be sophisticated enough to tackle such a gigantic part." She grimaced. "I was dead wrong. She was sensational; better than ever I could be and, apart from her acting ability, I think she was everything I wanted to be myself. I felt *soiled* in her company." She started to cry quietly.

Annie spoke quietly. "I think you do yourself an injustice, Annabelle. I think you are basically a very fine young woman". Annie shifted in her chair. "Now, did you have any of that so-called, Health Food drink last night, even though you did not go on?"

"No, but even if I were on stage, I would refuse to take that drink: that, so called medicine, which, besides all else, tasted like sewer water. I could never understand why so many of the cast drank it. I had pleaded with my father not to take it – or give it to others - as I believed, the drink could kill you - and it did…it killed Angela, and then it killed my father."

"Did you see Angela Cerney, drink the 'medicine'?"

"Yes, I saw my father pour out a dose for her, just before she went on in the mad scene."

"Thank you; that's all from me... Constable le Breton?"

"I think, Madam, you have asked all the questions I would have asked of Ophelia. I would like to ask Guilden-stern a question."

"Go ahead."

The constable faced the actor who, to his surprise, was older than he thought he would be. "Sir, did you take the drink that was being offered by Sir Harold Nicholson?"

"I think I would be dead if I had been stupid enough, or naïve enough, to take that poisonous fluid."

"But how did you know it was poisonous?"

"Don't be smart, sonny, or try to put words into my mouth. Let me make it simple for a young copper.

"One, I now know it was poisonous, as it has killed two people. Two, I didn't know that, when it was first offered to me. Three. I don't believe in Health Foods; it seems to me to be mainly fanatics who blather on about the benefits of their foods, and beverages. Does that answer your question?"

"Yes, but it still interests me. If you thought so badly of the Health drink, why then didn't you warn the young, innocent girl; she had no idea that that was not normally taken by the cast?"

"I am not here in this country of Kangaroos and Kookaburras – and not much else - to bother about the health of beginners in the field. It was immaterial to me whether she drank it, or not."

"Quite so, sir, thank you."

Annie turned to Jeremy, "Your turn, lad." Jeremy stood up.

"I'd just like to ask, Guildenstern, firstly, if his affair with Rosencrantz is over or not, as the stupid goat is now seeing that fake, Claudius. And, secondly, if he has made any progress with his pursuit of Hamlet, himself?"

Albert Fellows turned scarlet. Annie spoke quickly. "And Richard, have you any comments you'd like to make?"

The old actor was very angry at what had been said. He spoke first to Jeremy. "How dare you address an actor in that manner. You speak like a gutter snipe, something found in the sewer. I'm ashamed of you to speak in that way before a lady here." He turned to Guildenstern. "And you, to address a member of the Australian Police Force in that manner! If I were in his shoes, I'd arrest you immediately. If you are capable of that vulgarity, then you are capable of murder!"

Annie stood up quickly.

"Time to move on to the last group. Just wait here please; the next group of police will finish their questions. Thank you everybody."

They walked away, Annie spoke quietly, "Keeping your temper is never easy. The calmer you are, or seem to be, it rattles them more."

Before joining the last group, Annie stood with Jeremy and Constable le Breton, whispering.

"Well, what did we learn? I have to say my impression of Annabelle has changed considerably. I think she's completely innocent of the crime, as is the Ghost, Dominic Oddfellow. If that's the case, we can shorten our list of suspects. Do you agree, or not?

The Constable spoke first. "I agree with both, Mrs Watson. If that is the case, then if we include the death of Polonius, we have shortened the list by three people." He pulled a wry grimace. "I would like to make the guilty one, that supercilious beggar, Guildenstern, alias Albert Fellows, as well as give him a bloody nose." Both his hearers laughed quietly.

"And Jeremy?"

"I'm no good at this. I think they're all guilty. I wouldn't trust any of them."

"But, Jeremy, what do *you* think was the cause of the whole disaster? You must have an opinion."

"I think it's simple. A stupid Health Food Drink that was half rotten; it poisoned those who drank it and, I know it sounds crude but, it serves them right for being such naïve suckers for believing the opposite."

Annie moved further away. "Now listen carefully. We must walk on eggshells here. We are dealing with the great, one and only, Andrew, Hammond *hyphen* Oates. Now don't forget, this is a truly great actor…One of Britain's best young, Shakespearian actors…he is very, very intelligent; keep that in mind. See that he doesn't lead you; you have to lead him.

"Firstly, Constable le Breton, say over to yourself the names, so that the three words just run off your tongue as if, here in Australia, people having hyphenated names was something that happened every day.

"I know, Jeremy, you are familiar with this; we in Australia, are not. Constable, remember to only say: Mr Hammond Oates, that's all. For the love of God don't mention the hyphen.

"And two other things to remember. There is a period when Hamlet was missing from where he should be. It was only for about a minute but that's a very long time to leave a stage bare. We have to find out what he was doing during that minute. And we have another Player with us, this time, the son, Roland."

As Annie faced her third group, she was aware of great fatigue. She excused herself for a moment and spoke hurriedly with Mr James Cohen, the Australian theatre manager. She told him to arrange for the hotel for afternoon tea with plenty of sweet things to eat, to be sent as soon as possible to the theatre. Both the cast and the police were not machines; they couldn't just keep going without fuel.

Mr Cohen was a very sensible man; he said to just leave it all to him; he'd have it here within 15 minutes. He smiled. "You see they can't afford to upset us, or we'll cancel all future bookings with them."

Annie laughed softly. "Oh, I'm all for a quiet bit of blackmail when it comes to my food." And she hastened back to her group.

"I'm sorry, everybody, but afternoon tea will be here very shortly.

"Now, Mr Hammond Oates, firstly I want to thank you for that glorious tribute you paid to the amateur actress you were so kind to - both before her death - and afterwards. Very late last night I told the grief-stricken parents and siblings of Angela, what you said.

"They are wonderful, simple people. This child was the joy of their lives; they had been so worried about their daughter wanting to be on the stage. I think they associated the stage with all kinds of immorality and wickedness. But when she started taking lessons, with that Acting Studio, they began to see that it was, *or could be*, a rather wonderful career, dangerous, but all life is dangerous, and to an exceptional girl like the beautiful Angela, it could not really be a bad thing.

"Do you know what she did? She taught her parents the whole play! She read it to them at night and acted out different sections, always returning to the part of Ophelia. Believe it or not, before she was asked to stand in for the sick actress, her family knew her part, and all of them, including her parents, could recite it with her.

"I'm sorry to carry on about this, but this child was my neighbour, and I did love her dearly." She smiled at the group.

"Let's get this done with. Mr Hammond Oates, tell me,

did you notice anything that struck you as odd last night? Anything unusual or, out of place…"

The actor, dressed impeccably in a very expensive suit, and shoes worth a small fortune, looked directly at Annie. "Not really, mam; I was the only thing out of place."

Annie raised her eyebrows and opened her eyes wide in simulated surprise. "You were out of place, Mr Hammond Oates? … Please explain, I beg of you."

"Did you happen to notice that the stage was bare just before I met the ghost?"

"Oh, that! Yes, I did. But it was only for a few seconds, wasn't it?

The actor laughed softly. "I can only hope the critics thought as you did, mam. It was nearly a full minute."

"No! Really! As long as that? But that's not a long time, is it?

"To leave a stage bare in a very important play where it is vital to keep the action moving, is simply disastrous."

"I see. Thank you for telling me. Well, why were you not where you should have been? …Just a minute, let me get the place fixed in my head… …it was just before you met the ghost for the first time. I think that's right, but I could be wrong."

"No, you are completely right. You have a wonderful memory. That is exactly the time. Now, the reason I broke all the rules and rushed to the wrong side for a moment, I could see Angela and she was holding her stomach in what looked like severe pain. I rushed across to ask her if she was all right; to reassure her she would be wonderful – I thought it was just stage fright, and who would blame her."

"Mr Hammond Oates, tell me: you would have been the last person she spoke to on earth, what did she say? Was she suffering greatly?" Annie stopped with a gasp; she realised the implications of what she was saying… She then whispered, "Do you really mean to tell us that she gave that thrilling performance, *as she was dying?*"

As the tension grew, the group huddled together, in their distress. Roland closed his eyes tightly, Laertes had his arm supporting Rosencrantz while the constable and Jeremy half rose in their chairs.

The great actor's voice thickened and threatened to break. With a tremendous effort he managed to say: "I think that is the case, mam."

Annie was really shaken. She had thought that *could* have been possible. but hoped, desperately, it was not.

She quickly turned to the group. "Did anyone see Angela after her scene in the stream?"

All the actors shook their heads. Annie turned to the stagehand. "Jeremy, whose task was it to get Ophelia out of the stream, Was it yours?"

"No, it was no one's. Usually, the actress playing Ophelia would just get up out of the cavity as soon as the light, which had revealed her, had moved away. It never would have occurred to Charlie, or to me, to go to her assistance. It was just like getting up from a chair."

"I understand," replied Annie. "What about you Laertes, did you notice anything odd at all, of the performance last night…any other person, 'out of place,' as it were, or saying, or doing, anything that would give us a lead in this confusing case?"

Laertes frowned as he thought back on the whole performance then replied slowly. "I think, to be totally honest, the whole drama of what happened *after the play finished*, has so overwhelmed me, I can barely remember performing at all. I have to keep reminding myself that I was on this stage, in the play, last night…I was actually here. It doesn't seem real, now."

"That sounds honest to me. We don't go around analysing every action we do, or word that we say. But…"

Laertes interrupted Annie. "Excuse me, mam, but I have just remembered something. I don't think it's the slightest bit important, but you said…anything. Well, this is it.

"I was getting ready to go on for my fairly long conversation with Hamlet, when I saw Fortinbras - you know, the Prince of Norway – punching a cushion stage left. It was so odd. Usually, he's a very quiet and …controlled, individual, it gave me a shock, so much so, that I suddenly remembered it now, when just about everything else has left my head. It's probably nothing anyhow…"

"Not at all. Thank you, Laertes. Yes, it may have been anything from a sudden fear of the scene ahead, or even an inconvenient attack of colic… or… a vital clue that leads us in the right direction. Right then, anything else, Lawrence Toohey, otherwise known as Laertes?"

"Nothing, mam."

"Roland? What about you? Did you, observe anything that troubled you, or made you wonder?"

"I'm sorry, mam. I was so enthralled by Hamlet and Ophelia's performances that I had no eyes for anyone else, really." The good man bowed slightly to the lead actor.

"Now, finally, William Smithers, alias Rosencrantz, give me something, anything, *please*, and then we can have a cup of tea." Annie laughed gently, and they all smiled at the little joke.

"I'm really sorry, mam, I'd love to be the one who said, dramatically, 'I know who did the wicked deed,' but I don't. I was sunk in my own problems so deeply, that it's a wonder I didn't wreck the whole production. Sorry, mam, I have nothing."

"Right, we'll leave it there and have our tea. Thank you, gentlemen. I am grateful to each one of you."

Annie stood up and the men did likewise. They headed for the stage and the afternoon tea waiting for them. At the hastily erected table that was set up, Annie took a cup of tea, her eyes taking in the headlines of the latest publications that had arrived at the hotel: The first one indicated that the mystery had entered the domain of the academics:
SYDNEY UNIVERSITY PROFESSOR OF ENGLISH PREDICTS,
ROSENCRANTZ. GUILDENSTERN AND GERTRUDE SHOULD GO NEXT!
The second one was, perhaps the only true one so far:
THEATRE CLOSED:CAST IN HIDING IN HOTEL: TIGHT SECURITY. MASSIVE POLICE DETAILED TO MYSTERY.
The fourth paper made her smile:

HAMLET IN HOSPITAL: CLOSE TO DEATH
DISTRAUGHT WITH SHOCK

Annie, holding her cup of tea, then whispered to Charlie, who left the table and joined her a short distance away.

"Mam?"

"Charlie, a couple of quick questions, about Jeremy."

"Fire away, mam."

"You are the one who told me the reason why you had to plant Ophelia in the stream on your own, and it was that your fellow stagehand had come down with stomach pains and then diarrhea. Is that right? Did you actually *witness* this distress?"

"Well, I saw him groaning in the cubicle we share - which has its own toilet - then he rushed into the toilet and there were dreadful noises and more groaning and moaning from there. I left him pretty smart; I tell you".

"Is that the first time you've found him ill?"

Charlie shifted his feet uneasily and lowered his voice. "Mam, does what I tell you has to be shared with the rest of the police? I want to help all I can, but I will not put in my friends."

"Listen, Charlie, if the information has no connection with these murders, they remain private with me; if they are connected, I must report them."

"Oh, they have nothing to do with the murders. It's only that Jeremy has a drinking problem, and a few times I've had to cover for him when he's been on the booze."

"But this particular time? Was it just what normally happens when he's been on the booze?

"No, mam. When I went to collect him to help me with the body of Ophelia, I had never seen him like that before."

"Thank you, Charlie. Now go and enjoy your little break with a cup of tea, or coffee if you prefer it."

Annie smiled at the young man and was about to return to the table herself when she noticed that Superintendent Manders was beckoning to her, so hurried to his side.

***

As Superintendent Manders began to speak, Annie was aware of the severe strain this was on the relatively young man. She took hold of his arm and listened intently to his news.

"Mrs Watson, I've been notified that the compulsory Inquest on Angela Cerney, will take place tomorrow morning at 9.30am. I was told, confidentially, it will be a simple and easy affair. The findings have to be: 'murder by persons unknown,' at this stage; everyone knows that. They just have to jump through the usual hoops and, especially, as the new Company Manager, Mr Hiram Stotelmeyer, will be there – he landed about two hours ago, I believe – we have to make sure that all the details of the law are fulfilled, and *seen* to be fulfilled.

"You, and Superintendent Peters, will be called to explain your involvement in the affair; how you discovered the body; then alerted the police to lock down the playhouse. You both could be asked a number of questions regarding your intimate knowledge of the victim and, even some enquiries about the family of the deceased.

"The magistrate will be a Mr. Claude Benson; he's a sensible man. He won't drag out the proceedings, but this whole performance has to be completed. so that the body can be released to the grieving parents and the Funeral can then go ahead."

"Thank God for that, at least, Super! That will be such a relief to those good people at Bexford North. Don't worry about us; we'll be both there at the time you want us. But, Super, when will they get around to the coronial enquiry into the deaths of Polonius?"

"I was worried about that as well, Mrs Watson. It seems that, as there is the real possibility that there could be more deaths, it has been held over pending the work and reports of the police – at least for another week at least."

Manders lowered his voice: "Mrs Watson, another matter: Angela's funeral will be a public one, so Reg and Susan will need help in arranging it; they would have no knowledge of what it could be like. The crowds could be enormous…"

Annie nodded her head. "Yes, I've been worried about that. I'll see Fr More and get him to check with the bishop; he'll need help with servers, flowers. Singers, and so on, and perhaps, security to control the crowds…?"

"No, we'll provide the security. Every policeman we can spare we'll use for security; if more are needed, I'll get on to the Commissioner. These deaths have been headlines- news all over the world by now. The UK company is so famous it is known in many countries. I'll demand we have hundreds of police, if that is what is required. We'd be expected to do just as much for a stupid idiot of a Rock Star. They can provide the same for Angela."

The policeman, with an effort, wrenched his mind back to the Inquest; he informed Annie he would be sending Constable Sheridan to drive them to the Inquest. He reminded her it would begin at 9.30am.

Annie thanked Manders for his consideration, and looking around swiftly, to see if she could be overheard, whispered. "Super, we can't do any more today, really. Couldn't we send all these people back to the hotel and you could go home, have a good, big meal, then go to bed, and don't let anyone - anyone at all - interrupt you. In that way you will be fresh and alert for tomorrow - and all the horrors, it may bring."

The very weary policeman, smiled. "That's the best suggestion I've heard all day. I'll do it!" He moved away to get the whole proceedings underway.

***

The next morning, the inquest went off exactly as the Superintendent had foretold. After a good night's sleep, Manders looked his old self again. Neither Annie nor Peters were worried about appearing in court; both gave their evidence clearly and concisely. They were asked many questions concerning their discovery of the body in the street. Annie noted that both the Magistrate, and the *replacement* Company manager, from England - a Mr Hiram

Stotelmeyer - were astonished at the coincidence of two theatre patrons, who not only knew the victim, but also knew from whence she had come.

The magistrate congratulated both witnesses for their clarity, and for the very real assistance they had given to the local police, especially for advising the local Inspector, to call in Superintendent Manders, and his team, from Tavistock Police Station.

The autopsy report made Annie flinch, as it was revealed how much cyanide Angela had in her stomach. Dear God, how then, she wondered, was the girl able to carry on for so long?

Superintendent Manders gave his report on what had been done, by the police, so far, and explained the extraordinary difficulty they had, with so many actors and stage-hands: of how each actor was mainly concerned with his, or her, part. They had no time to study other actors, or were concerned with where they were, or what they were doing. They really only noticed this, if it impacted on their own performance.

That remark elicited a wry smile from the magistrate – he'd obviously dealt with actors before! He then consulted two legal experts who were with him. They spoke seriously together. Finally, Mr Benson, addressed the court.

"I wish to thank all the witnesses this morning. It has been a pleasure to me to find such intelligence and clarity in the reports you have given. In my opinion the case is in excellent hands.

"It is only necessary for me to state, officially, that in the opinion of this court of enquiry, the verdict must be that the victim, Angela Cerney, was murdered. She was poisoned by a person, or persons, unknown."

"The court rises."

***

Annie shook hands with the Superintendent, then was introduced to the new Company Manager, whose name she immediately forgot, collected Peters; then they kidnapped Constable Sheridan to drive them back to Bexford North.

***

They had the funeral of Norah Brady, to attend. They hadn't wanted Manders to feel that he had to attend. He had enough on his plate as it was; he didn't need a highly emotional crowd to deal with.

Annie thought that she and Peters would suffice to represent the police with, of course, the ever- faithful, Sergeant Clarkson.

That one, lone, local police sergeant, had carried the brunt of the horrors of the deaths of both Norah and Angela at the Forge. He had been The one stalwart shield safeguarding the Cerney family, from the insensitivity of the Press Reporters.

***

Annie guided Peters, not into the church, but into the small cemetery, by the side of the large building. As she did so, she thought they couldn't get away from, yet another, reminder of 'Hamlet' as they were attending a funeral, of 'Broken Rites,' as had been the case with the Ophelia in Shakespeare's play.

Annie was trying to explain to Peters, that in the eyes of the church, as Norah had committed suicide, she, therefore, could not have a Church funeral.

Annie and Peters, with Sergeant Clarkson, stood with the Cerney Family, at the graveside of their beloved Norah Brady. Annie held Susan in her arms, while Peters had his arm round the shoulders of Reg, the big, powerful, one-time, Blacksmith, who had lived in the same Brady house with Norah, since he was a young man.

All Reg and Susan's seven children were gathered around the grave, there was not one dry eye – they were all weeping, unashamedly, at the loss of their loved 'aunt' who had really brought them up; who, in many ways, was another 'mother,' to all of them, instead of just an *inherited* 'aunt' – the daughter of the late Nan Brady.

Norah had been retarded and had the mind of a nine-year- old child. She was innocence itself.

There was only the family present with, besides the police, Lady Penelope Sheridan from the Big House and a plump middle aged, but still beautiful, Florence Armitage – a neighbour, who was comforted by her tall, big son, now taller than his mother, and the, now grey-haired, middle aged, milk farmer, Daniel Kelly, the son of the universally loved, late Hannah Kelly.

The priest was an elderly man with grey hair. He knew the family well and was a regular visitor to the house. He knew the beautiful Norah well, and apologized, in his gentle voice, for this form of the funeral service. He spoke simply of this 'child of God' who, though afflicted, brought nothing but love with her, wherever she went. He said he thought it impossible that she could ever, *even conceive the concept of sin*. In his mind she was like the angels of God, and all who had been touched by her innocence, and her beauty, plus her child-like kindness, would agree instantly with him.

When it came time to lower the coffin into the grave, the task was handed over to the four sons, with Ben, the eldest, instructing the others in a quiet, but authoritative, voice, what to do; he made them lower the casket very slowly. When it rested on the bottom of the grave, the undertakers moved in and retrieved the ropes, and then stood waiting for the priest to finish.

As they all watched, with real grief, the grave being filled in, Sergeant Clarkson drew Annie aside. He looked harassed, and… also, strangely… *guilty*.

Annie, whispered: "What is it, son?" Clarkson was a young sergeant, and he knew Annie well. "Mrs Watson, I think I'm responsible for poor Norah's death."

"What?" she exclaimed in shock, drawing the young man aside from the group. "What do you mean? She hanged herself, didn't she? Please tell that was the case I don't think I could cope with another mysterious death this week." She reached out and took the young man's arm. "Tell, me, what do you mean? *Responsible*, how?"

The young policeman, with a tremendous effort managed to keep his voice down, also under control.

"It was this way," he finally answered. "I had to go to the house to inform them of Angela's death; the Super was out on another job. I don't think I'll ever get over having to experience, not only the grief, but also the incomprehensible nature of the death! This was Angela, their beloved, young, first-born child! What did I mean, 'she was dead'? The parents didn't believe me; I had to repeat the news a dozen times at least. The whole family was in a state of shock and confusion; they kept asking me to repeat what I was saying. They couldn't believe it was true.

"One of the worst affected was poor Norah. She held onto me and begged me to tell her it wasn't so. I did all I could - from all the courses we take on how to deal with this type of situation - and it meant nothing! She kept asking me when she would be allowed to see Angela again: she couldn't take in the possibility that she was dead! DEAD as people are dead, in the cemetery."

"The family were no help to me; they were each wrapped in their own tunnel of grief. I had to do something: I thought Norah would go into hysterics, in a moment and what would I do, then? ... I suddenly had this idea.

"I told her, that now, she need have no fear when she, herself, came to die, as the moment she woke up in heaven, she would see Angela waiting to take her into her arms.

"She then said to me words which I didn't take in; there

was so much noise with everyone crying and the father, Reg, out of his mind, smashing his huge hammer on the anvil in the forge. I simply didn't know how to control the situation.

"But... afterwards I understood what she meant when she said: "I didn't know that; then the sooner I die it would be better, wouldn't it?" And, I stupidly, and *criminally* said, '*Yes*."

He then burst out crying, helplessly. Annie moved her arm and put it around the man's shoulders and turned his face away from the other mourners. She nursed him, back and forth, as she would one her own children.

Annie then spoke quickly, but very quietly and firmly. "Listen, son. I want you to promise me *you will not tell anyone else* about that conversation - to *anyone at all*. In times of great stress, we all say things we later think we should never have said.

"You should not have been left to face that horrendous job on your own: you are a young man. You don't have the endless years of experience which harden a policeman to the horrors of what they so often have to face.

"You've had several days of unbearable stress and sorrow; Norah was not a stranger to you; you have known that glorious girl/woman, for a few years now; you knew her simplicity and - I believe - her holiness. I believe that she would go straight to God like a rocket, and I also believe that waiting for her, would be, her dearly loved, 'niece' Angela." She lowered her voice still further and whispered to the constable: "And keep it to yourself, but Father here, thinks exactly the same, as I do – in spite of the 'broken rites."

She stood up straight again and her voice was stronger. "Now, come with us to the local pub: our famous 'Sheridan Inn'. Tim Johnson will have our morning tea all ready for us. When we get there, I'll have a word with Tim and I shall prescribe a short, but strong, slug of whiskey. Come lad, they are piling into the cars. I'll come with you; we can fit a couple in, as well, can't we?"

***

Tim Johnson, the publican, stood waiting for them. Everything was ready; he greeted each, and every mourner, as they entered. He knew them all; he had been their publican for many years now. He, and his good wife, Betty, had loved the gentle Norah, and there were more tears and hugs, as the mourners were ushered into the main room which was set out with a wonderful spread.

Both Robert Peters, now a local himself, and Annie spoke to Tim and Betty, and explained that they could not stop as much as they wanted to; they had to return to the investigation of the crime, of the murder of their beloved Angela.

Annie drew Tim aside and asked him, as a special favour, to give a stronger drink to Sergeant Clarkson; he was nearly out on his feet, mainly due to what he had experienced by the devastating news he had to take to the Cerney family. She begged Tim to do it, surreptitiously, so that no one would know he was drinking alcohol on duty and advised Tim, for the love of Heaven, not to make it so strong that it would impair his work back at the station.

Tim Johnson was a sensible man. He knew if Annie Watson asked him to do this, then the poor copper must need it badly. He promised to do, what she asked and, shaking hands with both Annie and Robert, he went to join his guests, and surreptitiously, to do what Annie had asked him to do.

***

Arriving back at the Theatre, their driver, Constable Sheridan, found that the cast were at the Hotel; they would not be returning to the theatre again.

When they entered the hotel, they found the latest newspapers waiting in the lobby. They paused for a moment to see what the headlines had to say.

The first read:

POLICE SHIELD SURROUNDING MEMBERS OF
BRITISH CAST

They were dumbfounded by the next one - just off the press:

SECRET 'BROKEN RITES' FUNERAL OF MURDERED
ACTRESS AT BEXFORD NORTH.

How could they have known about this funeral? This headline paper had a by-line:

FAMILY CLOSE RANKS: REFUSE TO SPEAK

MYSTERIOUS FEMALE CRIMINOLOGIST BROUGHT
IN TO SOLVE MYSTERY

"Oh, no! Robert, now life won't be worth living."

They were interested to see that this was simply a 'wrap around' the usual morning paper, so it really was only the one page that had this information. They're being fed information, she decided, which seemed to be mainly, wrong.

Peters trying to distract Annie drew attention to a notice left for them. She read it with interest.

They discovered they were to find the actors in a section of the hotel which was also a small Theatre where they hosted small Theatre productions, and 'one-man' shows.

Entering the very large, attractive room, they found, not rows of theatre seats, as they expected; instead, there were many small tables and chairs, where the cast were sitting quietly.

Annie noted that the Players had moved some chairs so that they could all sit together, not with the other actors. Two young policemen were talking to the family.

There seemed to be police everywhere. Annie discovered Manders was trying a new tactic: he had all the police, regardless of their seniority, interviewing the actors with whatever questions they could think of asking.

It didn't seem to be eliciting much information but, Annie, approved of the novel idea. It gave the poor actors a chance to talk to a stranger, and a chance to put forth their own theories of whom they thought could be behind the whole terrible affair.

Annie's glance swept round the strangely quiet room,

with just a subdued murmur of the voices. She noted, in passing, with surprise, that of the entire group of actors sitting at the tables, there were only three of them with small glasses of what looked like wine, before them. The significance of what she was seeing, was not immediately apparent to her. Her keen eyes had noted which actors they were in the play: *Rosencrantz, Guildenstern and Gertrude.* She mentally said the three names to herself.

She turned her head away, then swiftly turned back alarmed. Something was wrong! Her eyes sharpened. What the hell was going on? Why are *they* drinking, and no one else? Like a shaft of lightening, she knew what was wrong:

The sequence!

SHE SUDDENLY WAS AWARE OF THE TERRIFYING SIGNIFICANCE OF THAT SEQUENCE OF NAMES!

That was too much of a coincidence. Something was terribly, definitely wrong!

She turned quickly to alert Manders and Peters, but saw that they were talking with the new Company Manager, Mr Stotelmeyer, their heads turned away, from the actors.

Annie raised her powerful voice. "Where did that wine come from? Why are only three people drinking?

"For the love of God...*Supers... look at the ones who ARE drinking!*"

The two superintendents spun round in their seats, staring at Annie, as if she had gone crazy.

She knew she was taking a tremendous risk, but she shouted at the top of her voice: "Don't drink that wine! There's something wrong with it. It could be poisoned!"

The senior police rushed to her. Annie ignored them and sent extra Constables to stand with the actors with the wine glasses. Peters was concerned for his friend. "Annie, Annie, Annie, it's only a little drink…"

"Robert, don't be an idiot." She turned to Manders. "Super, where's the waiter who served that wine?" He dithered, not being sure whether the woman was right, or not. Both of the men tried to talk softly to Annie who, impatiently, cried out: "Well, if you don't believe me, call for the police surgeon to come, at once, we might be able to save some of them."

"Save them from what, Annie…?" began Peters, when he was answered by a scream of agony from Rosencrantz, who rose from his seat, staggered in circles with his hands pressed first to his stomach, then to his head, and crashed to the floor; he was followed by Guildenstern. Both men had powerful voices; their dying screams were loud and horrifying. The constables, Annie had sent to them, were trying to help them – not knowing what to do.

It was too late for any human help.

Annie raised an ashen face. "Manders, get that waiter and that damn bottle he must have used. Get the hotel manager to take you to the man and, *DO IT QUICKLY…* he will not just sit on his backside until you are ready for him!"

Superintendent Manders, his face crimson, grabbed Constable Sheridan and ran to the outer office. Annie was about to follow him, when Gertrude screamed and fell forward over the table. Annie rushed to her and held, firmly, the hands of the terrified woman. As the suffering grew in intensity, Gertrude screamed again, and again, began vomiting, and then began the beastly diarrhea began. Annie moved to hold the shoulders of the suffering, shaking, dying woman.

Annie, cried out again: "Look! I can't hold Gertrude. Someone, please come and help me," To her surprise, it was Margaret and Sweetheart, from the Players, who came instantly to her aid. "Thank you," gasped Annie, "get those cushions from the bench and we'll make a little bed here on the floor by the chair; then help me lift her down." She was just about to lift the dying woman, when she was politely elbowed aside, and Hamlet, himself, then lifted the main weight of the very ill actor to the floor.

Annie cried out, in grief: "Gertrude is definitely dying." There was a cry of sheer despair by Annabelle Nicholson. "No, no, no, she's the last one I have…please God, no!"

"Come here, child," ordered Annie. The company 'Ophelia' came to Annie who urged her to kneel and hold the hand of the dying woman tightly. During the lapses of wrenching pain, Gertrude, opened her eyes. and seeing Annabelle, smiled a painful smile, then closed her eyes, but gripped the hand tightly – it was her last, and now fleeting, hold on life!

All affectation now gone, Annabelle was now, simply, a terrified, young woman, facing the reality of death, for really the first time in her life. She cried loudly, without ceasing.

When Gertrude had died, Annie whipped the tablecloths from adjacent tables and cleaned up all she could of the body of the now, peaceful, actress. Annie used the cloths also to clean her own hands and arms and took three more cloths for Margaret and Sweetheart, while Hamlet did the same. They stood silently, waiting for Manders to return.

Annie prayed audibly, with her arms around the two weeping Players, for the three dead, while Hamlet stood respectfully, silent beside her. She then spoke to the constable who had been with Gertrude when the wine must have been taken.

"Tell, me, Constable, how did the waiter get Gertrude to accept a small glass of wine? He must have said something to her to make her believe she *had* to drink; she was too fine a woman to just drink when her fellow actors were not offered the drink."

The young constable raised his shocked face. "I can't believe all this happened. To answer your question, I have been guilty of great negligence, as I could have stopped the drink immediately... but I never dreamt..." He was suffering from shock and looked as if he could well be going to throw up. He said, closing his eyes, as if in pain: "You see, Mrs Watson, the waiter said it was a special gift from the star, the actor, Hamlet, standing beside you."

"No! No! Using my name! He's a monster..." Hamlet cried turned to Annie, "Before God, mam, I had nothing to do with it!"

"Hush, son! I believe you; I know you had nothing to do with the drink, but I'm certain I know now, who is behind the whole affair." She went to pat Hamlet and saw the state of her hands. "Run along to the bathroom, son and scrub yourself clean, then I'll do the same. The end is in sight."

***

Back in the main office, the hotel manager had rushed to do as the irate policeman, demanded. He said the waiter was a casual, named Luigi Sonderello, and was an Italian. He admitted he had never seen the man before he hired him in desperation – he needed far more staff now the actors were there 24/7. He admitted he had taken Luigi without any references. However, he did know where he could be found now; that was in his own room.

Manders and Sheridan ran with the manager to the room and found it locked. Manders, in fury, kicked the door in. Standing with his back pressed against a window was a tall, slightly tanned man, who was still holding the bottle, clasped to his chest with both hands. He backed away, terrified, when the police barged in, then closed his eyes, as the superintendent shouted: "Get that bottle…Sheridan, GET… IT!"

The waiter, swiftly turned his back on both men and Holding the bottle up to his mouth, began drinking the wine in large, and gulping, swallows. With such a large dose of cyanide, the onset of death began quickly. Constable Sheridan managed to get the bottle away just before the screaming man fell to the floor in agony. Manders stepped over the dying man, ignoring his deadly convulsions, and began searching the cupboard drawers for any clues as to the identity of the unknown person, who had obviously paid for all this to be done, by the waiter.

All he found was a large bundle of money, in Australian currency, in the drawer by the bed. That was all.

Manders gave orders to his constable in a harsh voice: "Secure the room, Sheridan, then join me in the actors' Room. I'll contact the ambulance again". He turned away.

"I think we'll ask for a regular service; it could come cheaper!" He added bitterly.

Manders took the Hotel Manager back to the man's own office. The man was in a state of shock, so Manders sat him down, back at his own desk. He then pulled out the money he had found; he then gave it to the shocked man.

"This money belongs to the dead man, Luigi, so I cannot retain it. The dead man, your employee, will be taken very soon to the morgue. There will be a coronial enquiry on the death. You will be required to give evidence as to the hiring of this waiter, and also as a witness to his death.

"Both the Constable and I will be required to give evidence, as well. The findings will be, I think, 'suicide while being of unsound mind' – that's the usual practice. The man is dead, so all the court will be interested in is getting him buried.

"I want you to use that money – ill begotten as it was – to be used for his burial. In that way, the poor man will have a decent burial, and not be just shoved in the ground as a 'police removal'. Understand?" The man nodded and the police left for the big room.

Back in the main room, where there were actually two telephones, Manders rang for the ambulance, to take the bodies of the three men to the morgue for a full autopsy, and ordered, brusquely, they were to come immediately.

Annie then was able to inform him, that Gertrude had died while he was absent, so when the ambulance arrived, Manders sent Gertrude's body with the three male bodies, to the morgue, demanding a full and comprehensive autopsy to be done on each one - with particular emphasis on the stomach contents.

Hamlet stood silently, perfectly still, as the bodies were carried out, while Annie went to the new 'replacement manager', Hiram Stotelmeyer.

"Mr Stotelmeyer, would you tell the hotel manager that we need some strong coffee, or tea, with something bland to eat. I'd suggest something that had to be cut open, such as rolls. And, as quickly as possible."

The middle-aged man spoke in reply, as if he were waking from a nightmare. "I can't believe what I have just seen. God help you, Madam and all the police. I would have been driven mad if that's what I'd faced in this situation…I'll do exactly as you say. I have no suggestions to make at this stage about anything at all."

Annie's face was grim. "Well, I have another suggestion to make. Stay with the kitchen staff and watch them like a hawk to see if they do *anything*, or put anything into the food, that they are serving.

"In their negligence, they are totally responsible for their waiter, who has poisoned at least three people. Until that is solved, the Hotel is legally responsible.

"I'll send a Constable with you; a good one who won't miss a trick." She looked around, then raised her voice. "Constable le Breton, go with Mr Stotelmeyer to the kitchen and supervise, minutely, the afternoon tea. Ask about each and every ingredient used." The constable ran to Stotelmeher and led him to the kitchens.

Annie sat down, exhausted. Peters brought her a glass of water. She raised her eyebrows and said quietly. "This is probably poisoned as well; so soon, no one will be left, not even me…"

Peters mopped his brow. "Annie, once again you were right, and we were hopelessly wrong. I don't know how you do it. We see all that you see, yet you see what is wrong.

"I never could understand it in all our previous murders, and I'm damned if I understand it now." He once again patted his face with a handkerchief. "How do you do it?"

Annie sighed. "How can I respond to that? I have no idea. I cannot understand why the evidence isn't clear to everyone. I think it could well be that I'm just a frightful 'sticky beak', and want to know everything, so anything that is 'out of place', demands an explanation from me."

Peters sat down and closed his eyes – he was aware how old he was; he was worn out – so many deaths, so many murders – he was exhausted.

"Annie, we've been in some rough situations before, but nothing like this. This is murder on steroids – as the youngsters say today. Will anyone be left? We've got completely nowhere…we've finished our questioning…"

"Now, stop the negativism. We have advanced a little. We are now virtually certain the maniac who is doing this, is following the script of Shakespeare's Hamlet to the letter. He, or she, knows it so well, he knows the SEQUENCE of the deaths and, apart from Ophelia, he has been right on the dot with all the others! The professor from Sydney Uni was right: the deaths ARE following the deaths in the play and the deaths culminate in the death of Hamlet, himself. May God forbid!" She again made the sign of the cross and closed her eyes.

"Right," agreed Peters. "Then, if you are right and I have a horrible feeling you are, we have to find the actor who hates Hamlet, so much they are prepared to face death in trying to destroy him. They want him DEAD?"

Annie, again, closed her eyes; she too felt drained.

"Robert, I do think I do know now, the guilty one, or it would be more truthful to say, I don't KNOW, but I am guessing, who is the guilty one, but I'm not telling you just yet, as I might be wrong. Just give me a little more time. Not long, not more than thirty minutes, I promise you. I just need two more interviews."

"And, regarding the interviews, Robert, you are wrong; we haven't finished. You have forgotten, two vitally import-ant actors: Horatio and Fortinbras. Now Horatio had only a few minutes with me. You haven't interviewed him. Let's do them now; they might be emotionally unsteady, with all the drama of the recent deaths, and tell us the truth for a change…and there are the rest of the Players. I've only seen Richard, Roland and Margaret. I can't remember Cecily and

I definitely haven't seen Sweetheart – God help us! Fancy giving the poor child that name to cope with.!

"Listen. I want to speak to Hamlet first, then I'll speak to Horatio, then to Fortinbras in that order. You, and Manders take Horatio first, while I have Hamlet. Ok?"

Peters smiled. "Complicated, Annie, but that's as usual. Yes, it's OK. I understand."

Annie moved down to a table and chairs near the end of the room and Peters sent Hamlet to her. He was longer than she expected, but in a few minutes, she was joined by the leading actor who was carrying a tray. He placed it before Annie and then poured tea for her. She started to smile and spoke, tremulously, in her surprise. "You are not available for hire, are you, Mr Hammond-Oates?"

He mimed shocked surprise. "You didn't know this is what I do between roles? I have a wife and 17 children to support; my wife takes in washing by night." Annie was not behind in reacting to that speech. "And pray tell me, sir, does your extra work extend to poisoning, by any chance - perhaps poisoning by the hour?"

The actor smiled. "No, but I can see how profitable it could be; I'll think about it. I've learned a lot in my visit to your country."

"Well, it's not one of the careers we like to openly publish." She leaned her very tired arms on the table. "Mr Hammond…No, I can't continue with that.

"Look son, I am old enough to be your grandmother; for this talk, would you permit me to call you, Andrew?"

"Gladly, mam. I wish you were my grandmother. She is a

terror. She is the one who has forced me to do everything I can do: all the fencing, the gym work, the speech work, the memorising of huge, long, soliloquies as well as demanding high results from my schoolwork. I owe every success I've ever had to her, and yet we really are bitter enemies. We deal with each other with deadly, icy, politeness which I think is more frightful than open warfare. She made me do all the things she was forbidden to do when she was a young woman.

"My Grandmother told me she wanted to go on the stage herself, as a young girl, but her whole family were horrified. They identified the stage with every type of immorality, disease and the refuge of the very lowest classes."

Annie started to laugh, gently. "As the old song we used to play on gramophones, went: '*Don't put your daughter on the stage, Mrs Worthingham; don't put your daughter on the stage.*" Annie sat up straight and looked closely at the young man.

"Now let's get started, Andrew. I want to know about your friend in the play, Horatio. Is he really your friend, in real life? Remember I asked that when I first came to the Theatre and was speaking to the whole cast. When I say, your 'friend' I mean your close, *intimate friend, to whom you can tell all your secrets?*"

Hamlet started to tremble; his voice was not completely under control. Annie's eyes narrowed; she noted this with interest. Hamlet answered.

"I certainly have always regarded him as such, mam. I've known him all my life. We actually began at an acting studio together; we helped each other learn roles, and all the new stage jargon we had to learn in this mystifying profession. We learned the different positions of the body; how to use the body to express different moods and so on; then we'd work off all the tension in the gym with exhausting work-out sessions in our attempts to get the 'body beautiful'.

"Malcolm's and my family didn't mix – in reality, after my mother's death, my father mixed with nobody. My mother was a frail, beautiful woman who died young, and it nearly killed me. I wept buckets of tears until my father, using a long, thin, cane, threaten to flog me if I dared ever weep again. I have obeyed him to the letter; I have never cried once since that terrible day." The young man actually shivered, so vivid was the memory.

"The only one who understood what I suffered was Malcolm. He has been my one emotional outlet all these years." The actor paused and cleared his throat noisily. "I owe an enormous debt of gratitude to Malcolm."

"Tell, me, Andrew, about Malcolm's i.e., Horatio's, career. I am certainly aware of your stellar career, but I can't remember seeing his name on programmes, that we have had here from Britain. Or, in the truly wonderful, British films, from the marvellous J. Arthur Rank Organization, of the great Shakespearean plays, although I have seen you in two films, I think.

"When I was pondering your great career, I began to try to find out about Malcolm's career. I was surprised, as hardly a word was said about him. Yet, Horatio is a very fine actor indeed, and has a very important role here in this play, with the scene-stealing, truly envious, role, in which he has to say those tremendous, farewell words, when Hamlet dies. They are the words that ring in our heads, as we leave the theatre..."

Hamlet immediately recited: "*Good night sweet prince; may flights of angels speed thee to thy rest.*" He smiled, almost tearfully. "I have always hoped that there would be *someone, someday*, who would say those words to me, when I was dying."

The actor shook himself, closing his eyes tightly. When he began to speak, he sounded quieter and older than he was.

"I'm sorry I got side-tracked. You asked about Malcolm's career; well, it has not gone well. He is now scrambling for parts, no matter how small."

"Andrew, does he just lack talent? Or opportunity? Or has he, a bad agent? Or…is it, something else? … Oh, excuse me Andrew for a moment."

Police Constable le Breton, apologized politely. "Excuse me Madam, and you, too, sir. I'll only interrupt you for a moment. I just wanted to assure you Madam, that you hadn't lost the packet of lozenges; it was where you suggested I look. I put it in this small box I found. I tried to get it to you yesterday, but you had gone, by the time I found it."

He handed over the box to Annie, gave a little salute, and withdrew. Annie quietly said, "Thank you constable," nodded her thanks and turned back to Hamlet.

"You were saying, I think, 'it was something else', Andrew." The actor nodded, and again, closed his eyes briefly. "You see he has a drug problem and is, often, unreliable. I think, in this business, you can be as immoral as the old pagan villains of the past, and as long as it didn't impact on your acting ability, or your timing, you can get away with murder... literally, murder; but if you smoke grass, or if you are foolish enough to take any of the harder drugs, you are unlikely to turn up in time for the curtain to rise, or you would be likely to break down, and forget your lines or... perhaps worse still... you could, so easily, be ... subject to blackmail".

His voice faltered, then he hurried on. "A famous actor is in the position of Caesar's wife: 'he can do no wrong'. In many ways, an actor lives the life of a monk."

Once again, Hamlet closed his eyes. "Malcolm only got this job, as I insisted, he be given it. It is a great role, and he could easily do it; he is a very good actor. However, I warned him, if he mucked this one up – if I could even smell the cannabis, I would help him no more."

Annie undid the little packet the constable had given her and, without a word, laid the packet of 'reefers' on the table. Hamlet looked at them, then looked at the woman in front of him, his eyes wide with surprise. This unusual policewoman obviously knew all about Horatio's drug problem.

He looked closely at her and remained silent. He suddenly felt afraid – that he was coming apart.

Annie had begun to fiddle with the remains of a bun which was on her tray, tearing the bread into tiny pieces. The actor watched her uneasily. She kept her head down, but she could see the actor clenching and unclenching, his fists on the table. She suddenly made her decision.

Looking up, she asked suddenly and harshly:

"Andrew, you know perfectly well, Horatio HATES you, don't you? Head up; no pretending! …FACE THE TRUTH! He *hates* you … you know it, don't you?"

There was a muffled, "Yes … I do know; he… *despises me.*"

"Yes, despises you Andrew, so we don't have to find someone who hates you so much they want to kill you, do we? We've found him, haven't we?"

There was a whispered, "Yes."

"How long have you known that Malcolm is the killer… the monster of cruelty, who is behind all these gruesome murders?" Her voice softened. "*You do know, Andrew, he IS the murderer, isn't he?*"

There was a sudden wracking sob from the young man opposite her. He lifted up his head, with his eyes streaming with tears.

"Yes," he whispered. "I only realised that horrible truth this afternoon, with the seemingly, random, mass murders that we beheld in this room.

"I had wondered before, but I forced myself to ignore all the signs that pointed to him; this last hour I was watching him, and he gave the game away completely; he saw me watching him and he… … he…*smiled…mam…he actually smiled and bowed. He wanted applause for the horrors that he had done!*"

The great star, put his head on the table and wept, in

heart-broken anguish: his last, singular support in his life, now gone forever!

Annie stood up and came to stand in front of the actor shielding him from the rest of the room. She signalled to both Manders and Peters. As they came quickly to her, Annie pulled the young man to his feet and held him in her arms.

"I urge you both to treat this man gently. He has been under immense strain. He has identified the murderer for us. I want Hamlet kept in a safe house with complete protective custody, for the time being. God alone knows how many others are in on the plot – I think there is only one more. Hamlet only knows the actual murderer who planned it all."

She then whispered to Manders, "Super, arrest Malcolm Mc Dermic, immediately. Be careful, he's a killer: don't go near him without support *but get him before he leaves this room: don't let him get away.*"

Manders was shocked, Peters likewise. However, they took in the state of the actor, Hamlet, and Annie's complete conviction – it was clear that she meant every word that she said. They moved away to confer. Both men – to tell the truth - were afraid of contradicting Annie Watson. She had been right, and they wrong, too many times before.

But Manders and Peters, were worried. This was only one man's accusation as to the guilt of Horatio. They knew well that was not enough. They had to have *proof*. They went together to face the accused man who was smiling broadly.

Their doubts began to unravel, as the man began to laugh, then began to shout.

"You, poor, simple idiots! I fooled you completely. You looked everywhere, except where it should have been apparent to anyone, who had a grain of intelligence...or who actually KNEW THE PLAY!

"Horatio is never killed. He is one of the few left alive at the end of the play and that was what I want to achieve as well." He spat on the floor, then looked up as they stood before him. "So, what do you want, now?"

"A little question, Mr Mc Dermic. Did you knowingly and with intent, kill all these people, or not?"

"Are you stupid? Of course, I did, you simpleton. Killed them and enjoyed every moment of it. I've paid them back for refusing to give me the key role in this play; for only condescending to let me creep in like a grateful wet cat on a stormy night, because the great Hammond-Oates had put in a word for me... by his word...*his word! Good God...*

"He's an idiot; I taught him all he knows, and he has to cast a few crumbs to me, now, *his only ...friend!* Boohoo! ... Now he has no friends in the world...how sad! I've fixed him. The bastard! I hate him: I could do Hamlet, blind drunk, any day, much better than he does...he..."

Manders had had enough.

"Take him away, he revolts me," cried Manders, loudly, in contempt, turning away.

There was a short scuffle and Horatio was soon handcuffed to both Constable le Breton and Sergeant Watkins. They had just phoned the police station to send round the lock-up van, when it seemed to dawn on Horatio, what was happening.

He started screaming: "You fools, what do you think you're doing? You can't stop me NOW, I'm nearly there. I just want to kill Hamlet, the great star. The star! Dear God, he's the star? You have to be kidding! He's a fake; everyone hates him; his father doesn't speak to him; he lives with his grandmother… Lives with his grandmother! His grandmother!!

"He's like a little baby who hasn't grown up, the miserable slob. You know he should be a parson; he lectured me on smoking grass! The nerve of him: he's a nothing from a stupid family with a double barrel name. They're all mad in that family; he's totally mad as well.

"But he won't last long now. I only want a short while to torture him, then I'll show him how to use a 'bare bodkin'" He laughed madly. "A bare bodkin…that's funny, yes, I'll kill him that way; Shakespeare would be pleased with that when the great man – he lets me call him, William – hears that Malcolm Mc Dermic was the brains behind all these murders, he will remember the name, so will all the others. The name of Malcolm Mc Dermic." He started to giggle; it seemed he couldn't stop.

The prison officers had arrived with the van. They moved in and transferred the handcuffs from the local police to themselves and began to drag the hysterical man from the room. Horatio was screaming one thing, over and over, 'But I am Malcolm Mc Dermic'.

Hamlet stood beside Annie and Peters, watching silently, as half his life was being hauled away as well.

***

As the door to the small theatre closed, the sound ceased, and everyone left inside, breathed out in relief. Many men and women burst into tears. Both Manders and Peters assured everyone, it was now all over; they had been through a hell on earth, but the nightmare was now over.

The Superintendents decided that Manders should go to the local Police Station, with the other police handcuffed to the guilty man. He would officially charge the actor with Murder on several counts. He would sign all the documents necessary and then return to the Hotel. The accused actor would be kept overnight at the Police Station, then face a magistrate's court to see if bail was a possibility, or not, then depending on that decision, he could be removed to a security prison on the morrow to await trial.

Peters was in consultation with Mr Hiram Stotelmeyer, over legal assistance, for the accused, Malcolm Mc Dermic.

He also arranged for the deposition that would have to be made by Andrew Hammond-Oates - Hamlet - who had verified the guilt and made the accusation against the defendant, by ringing Sir Gregory Sheridan, who had been kept up to date with the case, through his wife, Lady Penelope and his mother-in-law, Annie Watson.

The great Prosecutor said he would be at the Hotel in less than an hour and would bring all the legal papers necessary. After signing the papers with witnesses, Hamlet could then be taken to the safe house.

***

When the arrangement for the legal work had been done, Peters and Annie considered the care of Hamlet - Andrew Hammond-Oates - in the safe house.

Annie suggested it would be less disturbing for the actor, if the safe house was close to Tavistock, so both of them could visit him frequently. He had no one else. Even the new Company Manager from London, was a stranger to him.

Annie understood the young man's intense isolation – he now had no one - and increased her hold on the young man; her arm firmly around his shoulders.

Peters and Annie, keeping Hamlet with them, discussed the locality of the safe house with Mr Stotelmeyer, the Company Manager.

The poor man was looking shell-shocked, but forced himself to listen to what they were saying. He thought it was not only practical, for Hamlet to be close to both of them, it was essential. He made it clear that all he wanted, was that the safe house would ensure complete safety for the famous actor. That was of paramount importance to the company. He would fit in with any plans they made.

When asked, Andrew – at first - expressed indifference as to where he was placed; he was still shattered by the revelation of the perfidy of his…friend. He kept muttering the line from Julius Caesar: 'et tu, Brute'.

After Horatio had been taken away, he roused himself and began to think clearly. He said he would be unendingly grateful, if he could be close to both of them. He then asked if someone could bring him some clothes and shaving equipment to the house. Annie suggested the housekeeper of the hotel: there must be one.

The Company Manager sent for the Hotel manager and demanded he produced his housekeeper immediately.

Mrs Jeffreys was a plump, sensible, woman and she took in the situation swiftly. She had looked after Hamlet and knew him well. More importantly, she knew his wardrobe; she would know what to choose.

She assured Andrew that she would do all he requested, and he need only let her know, through the police, when he wanted more arranged – such as laundry to be done - to just send it back to her. She would immediately see that it was done.

***

When Sergeant Watkins and Constable le Breton returned to the Hotel with Superintendent Manders, they brought the latest newspapers with them. The press was on fire again:

FOUR MORE DEATHS! WHERE WILL IT END?
ITALIAN WAITER CAUGHT UP IN THE MADNESS.
MURDERED.

Then in smaller print:

ITALIAN AMBASSADOR DEMANDS ANSWERS

Both Superintendents had to take Hamlet to the safe house. The parting with Annie was difficult. She held the young man, as if he were her own child, and promised him, she would be there to visit him, as soon as the police said it was safe for him to have visitors.

Annie assured the police she would be fine and asked them to leave Sergeant Watkins and two constables with her: that would be enough. She asked them to take that good Constable le Breton with them, to look after Hamlet personally.

She warned the Superintendents of Hamlet's shattered nerves and the anguish he had suffered; she begged them to be more than sensitive, to him; to be like the father the poor boy had never had.

Anne, as well as being a very compassionate woman, was also a very shrewd one. She added: "Take the Company Manager with you, so that there cannot be a word spoken of his being excluded, from the arrangements made by the Australian police."

As they were about to set off, Annie whispered to Hamlet, "Andrew, it will only be for a very short while, to a place where you will no longer have to look over your shoulder; where you will be utterly safe, no matter what happens. I assure you, my dear boy, the Australian police are very thorough. Now, just hold up for a little while longer. I shall see you when you are in the safe house, and believe me, I shall visit you as often as you can bear to see me."

The actor smiled and taking Annie's right hand, kissed it reverently. He then turned and walked to the police waiting for him; he walked as on the stage. It was a perfect exit, and Annie had a sneaking idea, Hamlet knew that himself which made her smile. He was recovering fast.

Now, she thought, I have to see Fortinbras briefly. Unless I'm totally wrong, he had nothing to do with it. Could be wrong, she cautioned herself. But there had to be another one who helped in the details. She thought she had a pretty good idea who that one was.

She didn't want to go there, but…she must…there's no way out now. But first: to deal with Fortinbras.

Annie was pleased that her estimation of Fortinbras, Alex Gardener, was correct. She described him in her mind as an 'amiable goof'.

She began by staring boldly at the man. He was young, of course, and good looking and wore clothes well. His speech was obviously trained, but nothing special, as was the case with most of the others. He looked, strangely enough, happy. She was soon to discover he was totally unambitious.

"You must have been disappointed, Alex, in only getting a very small part in this great play?

"Not on your life, mam. It suited me fine. I was running short of cash, and 'Hamlet' always has a long run, so I'd be getting a salary for weeks, possibly months. And, being such a small role there was so little to have to learn by heart. I've always hated that. No, the role of Fortinbras - whoever the man was - suited me fine."

"Yet you would have like to get the main role, wouldn't you?"

"No, truly I wouldn't. Always in the spotlight. Always watching the way you talk, walk, eat, always aware of the pressmen waiting to find you, looking dreadful, after a night on the tiles… you know what I mean.

"Perhaps, when I was seventeen, I might have dreamed of such things, but I was a stupid kid then who didn't know what he wanted to do, so took the one my sister talked me into trying." He laughed. "She said as I wasn't good for anything else, perhaps, as I was always acting the fool, I should turn that into solid cash, and study some acting. I rather liked it; you know, big first nights, free food, grog, and long sleep-ins, in the morning.

"One last question Fortinbras… Alex. What did you think of all the murders that happened here?"

"But they weren't real, were they? This is the world of make-believe. Nothing you see is real; it's all a pretence."

"But Ophelia's death?"

"Yeah, that really surprised me. I fell for that, I did. Then, it came all right. She was there again with her friend, Gertrude, a little while ago. I knew she was, OK, then."

Annie was stumped: could anyone be so stupid? She tried another track. "Alex, what do you think of our country. Do you like it."

The actor gave a huge smile. "Oh! I love it; I've always wanted to visit America. When we finish here, I'm going to have a look at Hollywood. I might see some of the great movie stars…"

Annie stood up. "Thank you, Mr Alex Gardener. Goodbye Fortinbras," her lips curled. "Enjoy Hollywood."

Annie raised her voice: "Only one more person to see. Jeremy, would you come …."

"*Quickly*," she shouted to the constables, "*get after him, don't let him get away…*"

She ran out into the hall in time to see the two constables chasing the stagehand up the stairs, which led to the roof. Annie thought: 'Damn the stairs, where's the blasted elevator?' She saw it and rushed to it and, pushing her way to the front of the people waiting to enter – ignoring their complaints, shouting out, 'Police' - ran to the controls and pushed number 5. The hotel was four storeys high, so No.5 *must* be the roof.

She knew the Hotel had a flat roof and that it was laid out as a garden for the guests in which they could relax, with views of the city before them and, even with glimpses, of the beautiful Sydney Harbour.

As she emerged from the elevator, she stood still, staring at the tableau before her.

The roof garden was surrounded by a safety wall, waist high. Sitting on the wall with a leg on either side, Jeremy Swift smirked when he saw the woman.

The two constables were standing helplessly 10 feet from the wall. If they moved an inch, the stagehand would immediately move his inside leg over the wall as well. If they tried to rush him, the man would be off the wall and fallen to his death, before the police came anywhere near the wall.

Jeremy looked up as Annie approached. He moved his leg to warn her. She ignored it, stopping about five feet away. The stagehand sneered.

"So, you found out at last, did you? Took you long enough."

"Not really, Jeremy. You left trances all over the place, but all that's not really important now, is it?"

"What do you mean, not important?" Jeremy was incensed.

"Well, now we're back to the eternal question, aren't we? The question, Hamlet asked, and the reason why this play is the most popular of all Shakespeare's plays."

"I don't know what you're talking about. What do you mean?"

"You are now showing us exactly what Shakespeare meant. He, too, obviously pondered the question that all people, with a functioning brain, ask, at some time, or other..."

"I told you. I don't know what you're talking about..."

"You are a liar and a coward, Jeremy...you are sitting where a sharp gust of wind would blow you into ...

... *WHAT?* ...

"*What would it blow you into, Jeremy?* Apart from death: of course, that is certain, and it's ... there... before you.

"You have to make the same decision, that Hamlet did... that everyone, at some stage, has to make...

'*...to be or not to be, that IS the question...whether it is nobler in the mind to suffer the slings and arrows of outrageous fortune...*' or, Jeremy, to just commit suicide and be done with it.

"Jeremy, Hamlet took from his belt a thin, very dangerous knife, which at that time, was called a 'bodkin'; Hamlet held the bodkin in his hand and knew that he had, there - in the palm of his hand - a way out: to end it all by suicide... all the loving...the betrayals, all the fears and all the disappointments... the sufferings...all of what we call, LIFE. Or, as Hamlet himself says:

'...*the heartache and the thousand natural shocks that flesh is heir to...*'

"But Hamlet pauses, Jeremy. He asks himself, what if there IS something beyond, when we cease to be? ...When we cease to live? ...Perhaps we start to *dream*...that could be absolutely terrifying? We couldn't control those.

"Jeremy, what if Heaven and Hell do exist? If life doesn't stop? If it just starts again, in a different place, and in a different form? ...

"I'm just an ordinary, simple woman, Jeremy, but I believe life does go on. I believe that when we were created by God, He created us to last forever.

"I know that life is cruel; it is hard and tough, and even our best friends desert us – as Horatio deserted you, when you were in the firing line. *Yet, it is still worth living*...for we can still DO something...how matter how little that is.

"I am nothing, but Shakespeare had one of the greatest minds of his age, indeed of all time, and he considered it real wisdom, and better to:

'*bear those ills we have...than fly to others that we know not of.*

Annie turned, as if to walk away. There was a plaintive cry from behind her: "Don't go! Missus, *please...mum... don't go!*

Annie turned back. "Tell me, Jeremy, was Angela difficult to handle when you went to take her out of the pretend stream, on your own?"

"You know?"

"Of course, I do, Jeremy. I just want to ask you to tell me whether it was very difficult, or not? I think it would have been difficult, as it is much harder to handle a dead body, than a live one. isn't it? So, did you find it difficult?"

"Yes, it was, a bit. I had to throw the body over my shoulder, and it was filthy with all the vomit and stuff. I had to have a shower when I got back to the cubicle and had to have it quickly so that the paragon of every virtue, Charlie, didn't see me...or," he laughed, "smell me!"

Annie continued. "And with all the poisoning, I suppose that was easy after you had poisoned the bottle of Polonius' Health Food drink. Where did you get the poison - the cyanide - from? Was it from Horatio?"

"Yes, he told me to poison the bottle of poor old Polonius, as he would give it to Angela and other actors; and he was dead right. I watched, as it killed Angela, then Polonius, then, later, Gertrude – but she only got a small amount; that's why I had to make sure she had more, later.

"Horatio then gave me more poison, to use to kill all the others. I gave the poisoned bottle of wine to Luigi, the Italian waiter, and bribed him – Horatio had given me a bundle of money - to take the bottle around, to just three people, as if he were just serving special drinks to them on behalf of everyone's darling, the great actor, the pretty boy, the bastard, Hamlet.

"I made sure Luigi knew who Rosencrantz was, and where he was siting. The same with Guildenstern. I made him also remember the sequence: first: Rosencrantz; second: Guildenstern, and an extra shot for Gertrude.

"I was glad Luigi committed suicide by drinking the poison. He couldn't talk then, could he?

"Hamlet was next on the list to go, but Horatio wanted to do that one himself. He fair hated the bastard, he did…

"I suppose you wonder if I'm sorry. No, I'm not! I'm sick of life." His voice started to break, and he began to cry. With a 'snuffling' mixture of tears and hiccups, he said as he appealed to Annie: "But, you are dead right, Missus, and also is Shakespeare… for:

'*Conscience doth make cowards of us all*… and…Missus,

"I'm …really…so afraid… to die!"

Jeremy brought back the other leg and came to Annie. He stood calmly, his arms outstretched, his eyes remained fixed on her, as the constables put on the handcuffs.

He offered no resistance at all.

There was a sensation of anti-climax as they travelled down in the elevator in silence: not one word was spoken.

As they arrived, they were met by a very worried group of police, which included Watkins and the two Superintendents.

Annie handed over the prisoner to Manders. "Take him, Superintendent Manders. Be merciful to him…please, I beg of you… be merciful to him."

She turned away, she just wanted to go home, and not see these people anymore: not be torn apart by them any longer.

Jeremy's voice followed her. "Thank you, missus… … thank you… mum! *You're just like my mum! My mum would've said all that you said! She was the only person who ever loved me!"* The poisoner then, knuckling his eyes, cried like a child. *"I'm sorry, Mum."*

Annie returned to the main room; sat at a table and, silently, wrote a report of all that had been said on the roof; it was accepted gratefully by Manders; she then left the hotel weeping. Others, seeing the expression on her face, cleared the path before her.

Peters rushed to her side and, thinking to comfort the woman, said to Annie; "But Jeremy's a murderer, Annie...a murderer."

Annie's response was swift and uncompromising.

"He's some woman's son. Even now, he cries for his mother; he's never forgotten the one person who loved him. He could be my 'Billy'. My son could have taken the same road that Jeremy did. Thank God for Jeremy's mother; she loved him..."

She closed her mouth and remained silent for the entire journey home.

Peters, without words, guided her to the police car which drove them both, silently, home.

***

When the exhausted Annie and Robert Peters, finally, each arrived at their homes, they found all the newspapers lying at their gates. Wearily they both picked up their bundles and silently went into the peace of their own homes.

Annie studied only the headlines. She sorted out the earlier ones and then the latest.

AT LAST! AN ARREST! SUSPECT COVERED WITH
BLANKET AS HUSTLED INTO POLICE VAN.
READ THE SAD STORY OF GERTRUDE, SOON TO BE
MARRIED TO POLONIUS:NOW BOTH DEAD!
Annie's lips twitched in scorn, at the next:
HAMLET RECOVERING IN HOSPITAL: PALE AND
THIN DEMANDS RETURN FLIGHT TO LONDON:
VOWS NEVER TO RETURN
YET ANOTHER ARREST: TOTAL SECRECY. PEOPLE
HAVE THE RIGHT TO KNOW. COMPLAINTS TO THE
BRITISH EMBASSY
HOSPITAL DENIES HAMLET EVER IN HOSPITAL. HE
HAS DISAPPEARED.
THE DAILY WIRE REVEALS TRUTH ABOUT
HAMLET: RETURNED TO LONDON SECRETLY DAYS
AGO. RIGHTEOUS ANGER FROM AUSTRALIAN
CITIZENS:
ANSWERS DEMANDED.
Annie, completely exhausted, emotionally, fell back on
her favourite lounge chair and kicked off her shoes. Now
roll on, blessed peace, she prayed. She pulled up a rug she
used in the winter and let her head flop back in the chair:
she was very soon, sound asleep.

**

It was eleven days later that the Requiem Mass for the
soul of Angela Cerney was held at Bexford North Catholic
Church.

A huge crowd had been expected, and duly arrived, eventually numbering nearly one thousand mourners. This included not only those personally affected by the tragedy – that included nearly all the inhabitants of Bexford North Village - but by many 'Theatre-patrons' who had been present at the tragic performance of Hamlet.

They had been shattered, as they had read the 'morning after' papers, to see that the actress who had thrilled them, with the finest Ophelia they had ever seen, had been murdered. A very large number of them were determined to pay their respects, by attending the Funeral.

The police, too, were there, as promised, in abundance as well. Bob Peters estimated that there could be up to 100 policemen on the ground. Many, of course, would be involved in the parking nightmare, crowd control, and general 'over all', supervision of the whole event, which promised to be the largest gathering in the history of the historic village.

The parents of Angela were overwhelmed by it all. They had never appeared in any public way, in their whole lives, and now, to be thrust into the spotlight – even to endure the agony of Television cameras monitoring their every move - was terrifying.

The children of Reg and Susan Cerney realised this, and surrounded their parents, trying their hardest to protect them in every way they could.

Susan was dressed in full mourning with a veil, for the first time in her life. Reg was wearing a new, black, suit. As the mourning car deposited them at the entrance to the Church, they stood, stock still, locked in wonder – totally stupefied - at the two, blown up photos of Angela, in glorious colour, which had been pasted onto boards eight feet high and three feet wide which were placed at each side of the entrance doorway, itself. There were, literally, hundreds of wreaths around the base of the photos.

These photos were from the Theatre and depicted the beautiful young woman in her costume as Ophelia. Cameras were produced by nearly all those attending, who had their cameras with them, to capture on film, a memento of this extraordinary, and heart-breaking death.

The Parish Priest, Fr More, was fully aware of what he was facing. He, being a shrewd, wise old man, brought in some of his fellow priests to assist him, so that everything could be done as perfectly, and as smoothly, as it could be done. He already had a well-trained group of young altar servers dressed in their black cassocks and long white surplices.

The church held 500, or there abouts. There was a special roped-off section which was reserved for the family of Angela. This was guarded by a security firm the priest had brought in for this task alone. The guards stood as sentries near the coffin which was raised on a trestle covered in wreaths in the centre of the aisle. The guards stood to attention for the whole of the Mass; no one at all was permitted to enter the area of the coffin, nor touch it in any way.

Strangely, in that special family area, a space had been left next to the father, Reg Cerney, which puzzled the other mourners.

Annie and Peters sitting in a privileged position, with

Sergeant Clarkson, who had received permission to sit next to Annie, estimated that nearly all the residents of the village, were present. Annie, too was veiled, not from choice, but on advice from Peters and Manders; she could be recognized as the 'criminologist spoken of by the Press.'

Lady Penelope Sheridan was there with her husband, Sir Gregory. Professor William Watson accompanied his mother - wearing the mourning veil - on his arm, while Peters – in his full-dress uniform - led in the well-loved, old Presbyterian minister, Mr Norman.

Superintendent Manders – also in his dress uniform - was given a special place of honour with his ever-faithful Sergeant Watkins by his side. The Elizabethan Theatre manager, Mr James Cohen, sat with the police Commissioner and senior policemen, who were all wearing their dress uniforms.

The constables were, in the main, consigned to crowd control and the car problem.

Mr Daniel Kelly, the very wealthy dairy farmer, owned most of the land still left in the village. He sensibly, opened a gate in a forty-acre field, which was both flat and dry, and made that available for car parking. This was a tremendous, and widely appreciated, solution to the car problem. Within the paddock, police acted as traffic wardens, directing cars to rows which would mean an easy exit, afterwards.

The huge crowd inside the church – both in the seats and along the sides of the walls had the excellent sound system, while the outside crowd had state of the art, loudspeakers, broadcasting both the Mass and the choir far and wide.

People outside stood, or knelt on the ground, or sat on makeshift seats; all were prepared for a long service; they were utterly quiet and reverent.

Even the TV Cameras were handled with delicacy and decorum: they were not, this time, looking for slips and mistakes, or humorous incidents; they were serious and treated the subject with due solemnity. They made sure they took the large photos outside the entrance, aware that their coverage of the funeral, would be seen all over the world in the night's news.

The slow tolling of the big bell, let the crowd both inside, and the hundreds outside, be aware the Mass was about to start. They had just settled down when there was a general stir, and a craning of necks, as Mr Andrew Hammond-Oates, the world-famous actor, walked up the aisle between his own, two large, security, men.

He bowed low to the altar and took his place – with utter serenity - in the place reserved for him, next to Reg Cerney, the father of the deceased, who immediately embraced him. It was immediately clear that they had met and that the father had come to care for the young, and famous, great actor.

As expected, every eye in the church tried to catch at least a glimpse of the famous young man. As soon as Hamlet saw the family was kneeling, he too, knelt. From then on, he watched what Reg did and copied him closely.

The locals were stunned by the glorious singing from the local choir. Never before had they been so good; more than good, they were brilliant. The local Church goers were feeling a little ashamed of their comments in the past about the poor choir: this time it was so glorious: they thought it sounded as if it were professional and were very proud of their local choir.

They were to discover, later, that the choir was, indeed, professional. They were amused to discover that six members of Opera Australia – four women and two men - had been present at the Elizabethan Theatre on the night of the tragedy and wanted to offer what they could to make this a special day. They offered their services, if they were wanted. Needless to say, the parish priest, snapped up the offer, with genuine gratitude.

The priest had a well-trained small schola, or men's choir. They sang the parts of the Mass that changed, while the big choir in the gallery carried all the rest of the singing.

When the priest climbed into the pulpit, Annie felt her stomach muscles clench in her apprehension. She was fearful for the elderly priest: he had loved this innocent, child of God – indeed, he loved the entire family and grieved with them in their loss.

Her fears were groundless. He spoke simply and with obvious sincerity and reverence, of the hope they all had of eternal life with God. People were expecting him to start talking about Angela, but he did not. He just mentioned as he was leaving the pulpit, that he had given permission for one eulogy; it would be given before the final commendation of the coffin containing the body.

The Mass was finally drawing to its close and the commendation of the coffin, which, of course, was still resting on the trestle in the middle of the aisle. The coffin had been covered with dozens of glorious flower wreaths. Indeed, flowers were everywhere. It seemed everyone had sent magnificent wreaths of startling beauty and variety. Now the guards carefully began to remove the wreaths and place them against the side walls. They did this until the coffin was clear of flowers and the incensing could take place.

The priest came to the foot of the pulpit steps and said, simply, "Will you please come forward, my boy." And to everyone's astonishment, the Hamlet of the play climbed the steps to the pulpit. He looked, for a moment, a little uncertain, and then began.

He used no notes; he spoke from the heart. As Annie and Peters listened to that glorious voice extolling the greatness of a young, village girl, her staggering talent, her innocence and her purity and her general, unaffected love for everyone, Annie started to cry and couldn't stop. Peters was much the same. Indeed, there was not a soul there left unmoved. Reporters, there among the crowds, began writing furiously. The eulogy would appear in all the newspapers the next morning.

The mourners followed the coffin, still with its guards, carrying dozens of wreaths, out to the cemetery next to the church, and there at the grave side, the choir sang the beautiful 'in paradisum,' as the priest blessed, incensed and sprinkled Holy Water on the grave.

Annie stood next to the most distressed of Reg's sons, Benjamin, while Hamlet stood, holding the grieving father in his arms, next to her. When the body had been laid in the grave, Hamlet whispered to Reg, then turned to Annie.

The actor took her hand and kissed it, just as his security guards moved in. They muttered: "It's time sir." And the great star was whisked away.

He left Australia for the UK to re-join his company, three hours later.

As soon as the grave had been filled in, the guards put back all the wreaths, so that there was soon no sign of a grave at all - just a mountain of beautiful flowers.

The crowd began to disperse except for the immediate family. They stood in front of the grave and said their final farewells. Annie stood with them, silently until they left. She looked up in surprise as Richard and Cecily York, from the Players, came up to her and timidly greeted her.

She responded by kissing them both and thanking them for coming to the Funeral. Of course, the whole family had come and Annie, and then Peters, spoke to each one of them. They informed both Annie and Peters they were flying home to Britain the next morning.

Annie asked her daughter, the Lady Penelope Sheridan, to take the 'Players family' to the Sheridan Inn and make sure they received special treatment by the publican, Tim Johnson.

There was an enormous feast of food at the Sheridan Inn. Tim and his wife, Betty, were flat out, with a large, new, hired staff for the occasion, to cater for the huge throng. It seemed that hundreds were lined up outside waiting to get in.

Annie spoke to Angela's parents and kissed them, then excused herself. She was aware she needed to go home, perhaps, do some heavy housework or, even better still, put on her old clothes and dig in the garden.

That was the best medicine.

***

The next few days were in the nature of an anti-climax. Annie worked tirelessly either in the flower garden, or the vegetable garden. She also found time to inspect her orchard which was just putting forth the first shoots of Spring. Soon, the whole area would be filled with the beauty of blossoms and the fence-climbing roses would soon be preforming their yearly miracle, and bursting into hundreds of wonderful tiny roses.

Peters kept her informed of all that was happening back in the Hotel, where the rest of the cast, had either returned to Britain, or else were about to leave. Mr Stotelmeyer was very busy and in constant communication with London, to discern what the Company, wanted done. It had been decided that the bodies of the dead actors should be returned to Britain, as they were well known and loved there, so that had been arranged, to the satisfaction of Mr Stottelmeyer and the relief of Superintendent Manders.

Malcolm Mc Dermic, as everyone expected, was refused bail, and was bound for Britain, as well, but he would go in bonds, and with prison guards, as he was insane. From the moment he had been taken to the Local Police Station in Newtown, after the discovery of his guilt, he had repeated, without ceasing, the following words:

'I am Malcolm Mc Dermic; I am Malcolm Mc Dermic; I am Malcolm Mc Dermic; I am Malcolm Mc Dermic...' and had never stopped saying those words, even when eating.

He seemed to have gone completely crazy. The jailers had to move him to a cell in an isolated section; he was driving the other prisoners in their cells, mad, with the endlessly repeated words. On advice from Sir Gregory Sheridan, the Company Manager brought in Specialists in this field of medicine, and they all had agreed it was utterly genuine; it was not possible to keep that up for twenty out of the twenty-four hours of a day. They had tried drugs, even ECT, but nothing made any difference. As soon as he woke, he would start again on his mantra. It had never altered.

At a special court hearing, Malcolm Mc Dermic had been declared unfit to plead on the grounds of insanity. He was then transferred to London, certified as insane.

Annie had to renew her involvement with the murders, when Jeremy Swift came up for trial.

The Company determined that the trial should take place in Australia, as the main witnesses to his confession were from there. Annie and the two Constables had to re-live that dreadful scene on the roof of the Hotel, as they recounted to the court what had happened there.

In court, Jeremy had pleaded guilty immediately, and the Jury were only away the minimum official time, before they reached the same verdict. He was given a prison sentence of 29 years.

After the sentence had been given, the British Government demanded he be brought back to London to serve his sentence, so Annie only saw the convicted man, briefly, before he was taken away. The visit was a draining emotional experience for Annie, but she obtained, from Jeremy, his mother's address and duly wrote to the poor woman about her wayward son.

Mrs Swift had been in anguish over her best loved child and cherished the letters from Annie. The mother never ceased in her visits to her son until she died. It was then, that Jeremy was permitted to write to Annie twice a year.

Eventually the whole cast, alive and dead had been sent back to Britain, together with Mr Stotelmeyer, and a very relieved Superintendent Manders, with his entire crew, were able to return to the relative peace of Tavistock.

***

A week later, after perusing the newspapers, Annie with a determined step in her walk, went to visit her neighbour, Robert Peters. As soon as he saw the newspaper in Annie's hand, he backed away, saying,

"No, no, no, NO! ANNIE, NEVER AGAIN!"

Annie, of course, took no notice. "Now I've decided…"

"Just a minute, YOU decided? I thought this was a co-operative affair. I have a say and, my 'say' is: Never. Never, again! Full stop!"

"Just a minute, sonny. Now you haven't even heard what I'm proposing. Now, just be quiet for a moment. I can understand you are a little put off the Classics - for the time being - but what about comedy?"

"Such as?"

"G&S."

"Which one?"

Annie started to sing:

"Are you old enough to marry do you think? Won't you wait until you're eighty in the shade? There's a fasciation frantic, in the ruin that romantic. Do you think you're sufficiently decayed?"

Peters laughed: "That's 'The Mikado': the best of the lot! So, we're going from, Shakespeare to Gilbert and Sullivan. That's from, the Eiffel tower, to the basic rotary clothes hoist! Well, we could use that very English/Australian expression to sum it all up:

'*From the sublime to the gorblimey*'.

Right, get the tickets! I'll go! Count me in!"

***

END NOTES:

[1].The 'Elizabethan Theatre' was a real live Theatre in New-town, Sydney. Until the Sydney Opera House opened in 1973, the Elizabethan Theatre was large enough to use for all the great productions sent to Australia from the UK. It had been, previously, a very large Movie Theatre which had then been called, the 'Majestic'.

The Elizabethan Theatre burned to the ground in 1980

[2].There is no Regent Hotel in Newtown

[3].'Bexford North': is a fictionalized version of an upper North Shore Sydney suburb.

THE POLICE

LOCAL
Local: Inspector Ted Scully
Local: Constable Mark le Breton

TAVISTOCK POLICE UNIT:
Superintendent Manders
Inspector Watkins
Sergeant Clarkson
Constable Bernard Sheridan
Sergeant Clarkson: Left at Tavistock Police Station to deal with the parents, & Aunt, of ANGELA